HAVEN 7
by Misty Vixen

D1528053

CHAPTER ONE

"Have you thought of a name yet?" Ashley asked.

David looked over at her as they stopped momentarily among the lush foliage, coming to stand on a small hill that offered them a better look into the forest that surrounded them. She looked radiant in the golden sunshine streaming down from above, filtering through the leaf-heavy branches that swayed gently in the breeze. She wore a simple, form-fitting tanktop and a pair of cargo pants ripped off at the knees.

With a combat knife on one hip and a pistol on the other, she looked like Ellie.

Which made sense, given how close they were nowadays.

"We're still batting that around," David replied.

"How far along now is she?"

David thought about it. It had been about three and a half months since they had dealt with the viper threat, helping the squids, and bringing Lara over to their group. Which meant that it was just about now becoming summer, and that Cait was…

"About six, six and a half months," he replied.

"Getting closer," Ashley murmured.

"Yeah."

"You scared?"

"I mean, yeah."

She sighed. "I understand. I don't have kids, I don't want any, but...you know, there's my little brother to worry about."

Distantly, from somewhere up ahead, they heard a gunshot. It echoed over the landscape. "We should keep moving," David said.

"Yeah."

They resumed their journey, heading northeast. They were heading towards the quarry. The last time David had been up this far, and so far really the only time as far as he could remember, was during the incident with the stalkers. Ashley had been out exploring the night before, going solo since Ellie had pulled guard duty, and had heard a few gunshots coming from the area.

She had meant to investigate, but a pack of stalkers had driven her off and it was already getting to be towards nightfall, so she'd headed home with intent to investigate the next day. And so David had agreed to go with her and check it out.

There was another reason he had agreed to go.

"Ashley..."

"Yeah?"

"Have you been avoiding me?"

She didn't respond for a few seconds. The only sound was their boots, moving through the underbrush, and the trees swaying in the wind.

"Kinda," she admitted finally.

"Why?"

She sighed softly. "I...don't know."

"I think you do."

Another few seconds went by.

"I guess, I'm a little jealous," she said finally.

"What? Why?"

"You and Ellie are...*really* close. Like *really* close. I mean, it didn't bother me as much before, but we're...kinda serious now, you know?"

"Yeah," he murmured, he did know. In the months that had followed the viper incident, there had been some fairly successful attempts to add on to Haven.

There had been some room in the front corners of the campgrounds, just enough open space for a few more structures. During the spring, they'd managed to gather enough lumber and construction material from across the region to build three buildings.

One took up one of the entire areas and served as a kind of boarding house, a two-story structure that sported a dozen small bedrooms. Evie had overseen the project, working with a few people who knew about construction, and she had envisioned it as a place for people to stay overnight if they were passing through, or even for a few days.

The other area housed a pair of structures closer to traditional cabins, though smaller. Ellie and Ashley now lived in one of these buildings, having grown close enough that they felt comfortable doing so. Besides having a romantic (and highly sexual) relationship, they also had taken on a sort of apprentice-mentor relationship, as Ellie was teaching her how not just to survive but thrive. In fact, she had taken to giving lessons to anyone who wanted them in the village.

But he and Ellie had only grown closer since her return to Haven. Although she wasn't exactly a part of the four-way relationship he shared with Cait, April, and Evie, she might as well have been. He and she and Cait were extremely close, to the point where they regularly told each other they loved each other.

He could see how that might be difficult for Ashley.

"I mean, I'm willing to listen, to work with you..." he said.

She sighed heavily. "That's the thing! What can I do? What can I ask for? You two love each other! What do I ask? 'Stop loving each other'? That's completely unreasonable."

"I'm...sorry," he managed. In that moment, he wished he was somewhere else, because damn was this uncomfortable. But this was exactly why he had come along, because it had become obvious that something was going on with Ashley, and he had been determined to find out what. He'd figured it was something like this, but how to fix it?

"I know. Fuck, I'm sorry for feeling this way," she muttered. "It's stupid. I know Ellie loves me. She moved in with me. I didn't think she'd do that for anyone. She spends time with me, helps me, goes on adventures with me, and I know what a big deal that is for her. She's used to being a loner. I can tell this is...stressful for her, sometimes. It isn't what she's used to."

"I think you might be worried about something else, Ashley," David said.

She looked at him. "What do you mean?"

"I don't think you're jealous of me or Cait. I mean, okay, I *do,* but I don't think that's what's causing you so much grief. I think you're scared that you're going to wake up one day and find Ellie has disappeared," he replied quietly.

She stared at him for a moment longer, then she looked away. They walked in silence again for a few moments.

"I guess you're right," she whispered. "I guess...I kinda latched onto the jealousy, because I *am* scared of that. I have nightmares about it, sometimes. And sometimes Ellie gets up before I do, and she's so quiet, I'll just wake up and she's gone, and I panic..."

He stopped and she stopped with him. David stepped closer to her and opened his arms in offering. She hesitated for just a second, then hugged him tightly. "I'm sorry," she groaned.

"It's okay," he replied, hugging her against him. "I know exactly how you feel, actually. I mean, I was there when she *did* leave last time. It was awful. I was sick to my stomach for days. And, I mean, I'm not *trying* to interfere–"

"I know!" she groaned, stepping away. "I know, I'm being a bitch."

"I didn't say that. I wasn't trying to imply–"

"Ugh, you're so fucking reasonable," she growled.

"Is that...a problem?"

She laughed and shook her head. "No, David, just..." She looked at him and let out a long sigh. "I guess my mom was right about me. Sometimes I just want to fight. Which is stupid." She stepped closer to him again and put her hands on his hips. "You're a really good friend. I want to make sure you know that. And just, you know, a good guy. I know why Ellie likes you so much. And I want you to know that I actually really like you, too."

He chuckled. "I had a suspicion."

"Oh really? Could it be those times I fucked you?" she asked, smirking.

"That might have tipped me off," he replied.

They stared at each other for a moment, an electric spark of lust passing between them. She looked a lot different now. She'd grown her blonde hair out over the winter and spring, and last month she had shaved half her head, and now kept it shaved. It gave her kind of a wild and crazy appearance. She was sporting a heavy tan now and she'd bulked up a little bit.

When he had first met her, she'd been pretty skinny, but now she had some muscles. Now she had a lean, cut look to her. One point, a few weeks ago, staring at her as she chopped wood outside of Haven, he had suddenly understood what people meant about him looking older.

When they met, she looked like a teenager or someone in their early twenties. Now she looked a decade older, more mature, maybe harder, rougher around the edges. The way she moved now, it reminded him a bit of Ellie and Cait.

"We should have sex," Ashley said suddenly.

"Here?" he asked.

She opened her mouth, then another gunshot sounded, a bit closer this time. She sighed. "Okay, later," she said, turning and resuming her walk. He hurried after her. "After we figure out what's going on over there. Then we'll go back to my place and fuck. We haven't fucked in forever."

"Not my fault," he murmured.

She heaved a sigh. "I *know!*" She shook her head. "Let's just...focus on this. They've gotta be in the quarry, whoever they are."

"You think so?"

"Yeah, that's the only thing that's in this direction, really."

"God, I hope it's not a bunch of assholes looking to wreck our shit."

"Yeah…"

She frowned, and he knew she was likely thinking of the same thing he was: Lima Company. Although there had been no hostility between the two groups, Stern had made it apparent that he wasn't interested in working directly with them any longer. Especially now that his second in command had left him and joined Haven.

David was very glad to have Lara around, for a

number of reasons, but he wished it hadn't been done out of frustration and anger. Not that he could blame her. Stern had gone back on his promise to help the squids, instead trying to push the responsibility solely onto David and his own group.

And it wasn't like he minded doing it so much as he was extremely disappointed in Stern's own dereliction of duty.

He was at least glad that his relationship with the other three groups in the territory was still going strong. He still traded regularly with the fishermen and the farmers, and the doctors were strong allies by this point. He was sure that if they had room, they could convince them to move into Haven. But that was another problem for another day.

Abruptly, the trees and the dense foliage fell back, and he and Ashley came out onto a strip of land that ended abruptly ten feet ahead of them. They carefully approached the edge and as they did, found themselves looking out over the quarry.

Immediately, David's question was answered. Off near the other end of the quarry, where a gentle slope in the land led down into it, he spied a collection of a dozen or so tents and a large group of people moving around them.

"Well, holy shit," Ashley muttered.

David pulled out his binoculars and took a look. "They don't *look* like assholes."

"Oh yeah? How can you tell?"

"They've got kids with them. They look more ragtag than anything else. Like they picked up random people from here or there. It looks...kinda peaceful. Or as peaceful as it gets."

"The thieves were pretty ragtag."

"Yeah, but you could tell they were all from the

same group."

"Yeah...so now what? You're the boss."

He lowered the binoculars and glanced at her. "Oh, so you'd actually listen to me?"

"Provided you don't give dumbass orders," she replied. "I think you're doing a good job helping run Haven with Evie and Cait and the others."

"Well thank you. Now, we carefully introduce ourselves. Try and figure out their intent. Kinda wish we had more people...actually, maybe we should run back and get more," he said. "It'd be nice to have a sharpshooter covering us just in case."

"Yeah, can't argue with that logic," Ashley murmured. As he began to turn away, Ashley grabbed his arm. "David, look."

He turned back and his heart skipped a beat. Half a dozen large, dark figures were sailing overhead now. Hunters. He heard several people scream. At the same time, he caught a wave of movement by the treeline over on that side of the quarry. Pulling the binoculars back up, he saw what was causing it: stalkers. A few dozen of them.

"Shit, we have to help them," he said, replacing the binoculars and hurrying off.

Ashley silently followed after him. They began sprinting along the path that ran alongside the quarry, careful to keep their distance from the edge. Fuck, what a shit way to go. After everything he'd survived, how damned awful would it be falling to his death? David kept running, keeping an eye on the situation as it developed.

The people were fully aware of the monsters now, both above and on ground level, and he could see them scurrying to set up defenses. Judging from how quickly they were doing it, they seemed pretty well-prepared, although they didn't have the most ideal of setups for something like this.

Gunfire rang out as they took shots at the hunters wheeling overhead and opened up on the stalkers sprinting down the slope into the quarry.

David and Ashley ran for all they were worth, and by the time they finally reached the other end of the quarry, his lungs and muscles were beginning to burn.

"Stay up here," he gasped, skidding to a halt and surveying the situation again.

A lot of stalkers had been put down already, but apparently all the ruckus had garnered the attention of a pack of wildcats and now *they* were coming down. Three of the hunters had been killed, but the other three were fast, and they were dive-bombing again and again, shrieking wildly, making grabs for the survivors trying desperately to hide and fight.

"You've got the rifle, take down those fucking hunters, Ashley!" he snapped when she began to argue.

"Fuck, fine!" she growled, pulling out her scoped rifle and getting into position.

David brought his pistol out and started running down the slope, towards the encampment. As he got within shooting range, he screamed, *"Friendly, coming in! Friendly, coming in hot!"*

He had no idea if they could hear him over the screaming and the gunfire, but he had to try. David got within a few dozen meters of the onrushing stalkers and wildcats, trusting Ashley to take out the hunters, or at least dissuade them from trying to murder him.

He skidded to a halt and opened fire. The first two shots took a wildcat through the skull and splattered its rotting brains across the horde. It rag-dolled and rolled a few times down the incline as the life left its body in a hurry. He popped off more shots, missing two, scoring another headshot through a stalker, and pumping two rounds into another wildcat's chest. That got their attention.

A pack of wildcats peeled off from the horde and began sprinting towards him with a terrifying speed. As he took aim, David found it easier than he would have a few months ago to steady himself. Apparently all the practice was paying off. He opened fire on the rampaging targets, the pistol jerking in his hand against the backdrop of gunfire roaring around him.

The lead wildcat's head snapped back in a spray of bone and blood and brains, and it flopped to the ground, tripping up another one of them. David snapped to the right and fired twice more, the first shot going through a neck covered in patchy, matted fur, the second turning a wide, empty black eye into a geyser of old blood. He emptied the pistol putting down the onrushing undead.

Without missing a beat, he ejected the spent magazine and slammed a fresh one in.

"*DAVID!*" Ashley screamed distantly behind him.

He looked around, knowing something had to be about to attack him, but saw nothing. Then he looked up. No, not attack him, land on him. One of the hunters Ashley had appeared to have killed was falling right towards him.

He dove out of the way just as five hundred pounds of dead meat smashed into the ground with a resounding crash. Picking himself up off the ground, David looked around. He saw a few more stalkers coming his way, but the numbers were finally thinning out. Overhead, only one more hunter circled, and Ashley was on it.

He kept up a steady rate of fire, punching bloody holes into the malformed bodies of the undead as they came at him, and between himself, Ashley, and the people at the encampment, they managed to put down the last of the undead.

As David reloaded again, he took a look at the camp, trying to figure out whether he needed to run or–

A bullet shrieked past him, barely missing his leg, and he cried out and dove back behind the dead hunter. "Friendly!" he screamed. "Fucking *friendly!*"

"Val! Fuck! Stop!" a voice yelled, a woman's voice.

Another woman's voice, gruff, spoke up. "Who the fuck is out there?!"

"My name's David! Will you *please* not shoot me!?" he called back.

"No promises! What do you want!?"

"Val! *Fuck!*" the first voice snapped.

David looked up, frustrated that he didn't have anywhere to go. No doubt Ashley was covering him but there were a few dozen people over there and this was a pretty open space. He probably hadn't seriously thought this out. Then again, that was the problem with wanting to help people in desperate situations.

He heard arguing between the two voices, though he couldn't make out most of the words. Finally, the first voice, one that sounded more reasonable, called back to him. "David, was it? We won't shoot you! Thank you for your help!"

Sighing, deciding to take her at her word, he slowly stood up. He could see two figures standing by one of the tents nearest to his position now, maybe thirty meters away. One slim and one larger, though not tall enough to be a goliath.

Just a tall human. The tall one carried a scoped machine gun and looked prepped for war. She reminded him of Katya or Vanessa. The other woman seemed almost the opposite: slim, average height, kind, maybe a little out of her depth, judging by her expression. But she seemed reasonable, at least.

"It's David," he said.

"Can we talk?" the first woman asked.

"Only if your friend comes down off that hill and stops covering us with that rifle," the second woman said firmly.

David turned and waved to Ashley. After a moment, she stood up and started coming forward. He waited until she had joined him and then the two came towards the encampment. They stopped a respectable distance away.

"Who are you?" the second woman asked.

The first woman sighed. "Stop being such a fucking bitch, Val," she growled. "My name is Lori," she said, smiling winningly at them both. "I am the leader of this group. Valerie here is my second in command. She—"

"Makes sure you don't fucking die," Valerie grunted.

"Quite."

"My name is David, this is my friend Ashley. We're from a settlement that I help run called Haven, a little ways south of here. We heard gunshots and came to investigate. What's, uh, your situation? Are you passing through or looking for a place to stay?"

"Well—" Lori began, but Valerie cut her off.

"What's it you?" she asked.

"We're in a position to offer assistance if you

need or want it," David replied.

"Why?" Valerie pressed.

"Because I'm fucking nice," David replied.

"Bullshit."

"Val! Go...check on the others," Lori said, turning to her and staring up into her face. "You're pissing me off and being extremely fucking rude."

"Do I really have to remind you how the last 'interaction' went?" Valerie replied, but she turned and left, heading deeper into the camp.

Lori walked a few steps closer. "I'm sorry about her."

David sighed and shook his head, making himself calm down. "No, it's fine. I get it. There's a lot of assholes in the world and talk is cheap."

"Well you *did* help us, but...I must admit, we've had a run of very bad luck recently. We've been hassled and hunted by some group for the last forty miles."

David frowned. "Really? What were they like?"

"They wore leather armor painted black and they were pretty...tenacious. And vicious. When we first ran into them they pretty much tried to demand our unconditional surrender. They wanted all of our resources and some of our people. They were in a position to take it, too. We got lucky. A pack of giants was wandering nearby and got drawn in by the shouting. We fled, but they kept finding us. It's been a week since we've seen them, though...I hope they haven't followed us." She sighed and appeared to collect her thoughts. "But, um, thank you. Both of you. That was good shooting, and very helpful."

"You're welcome," David replied. "So what *are* your plans?"

"I don't know," she admitted after a moment.

"We're running low on supplies. We've set up camp here with the intent to hunt and gather some resources, but, God, I think everyone's just tired of moving..."

David stared at her. She *looked* tired, and frightened. Also, very pretty. Medium height, probably a little under average weight, chin-length blonde hair, soft brown eyes. She looked really good in her jeans and t-shirt.

"I want to help," he said. "Last winter, me and some very close friends built a whole settlement on the foundation of helping people. So, if there's anything I can do..."

Lori pursed her lips, staring at him. He had to admit, she didn't have a great poker face. She looked desperate and wasn't doing a good job of hiding it. He had the idea that they were worse off than she'd like to admit.

Finally, she stepped a little closer. "We could *really* use the help," she said, her voice low. "We have several people sick and now hurt, we're very low on food and water and are basically out of medicine. There's close to forty of us..."

"Fuck," David whispered. "That's...okay. That's a problem, yeah."

"Anything you could do..."

David considered it for a moment. He glanced at the sky and made a quick calculation. It was still before noon. With how long the days were now, he could definitely go home, get some people and even just a basic care package, and come back. He looked back at her and nodded.

"All right, listen, I'm going to go put together a care package of supplies. Food, water, medicine, ammo, and a few medical personnel to come and look at your people."

"If you could..." Her breath caught and she cleared her throat. "If you could do that, it would be *extremely* helpful. It's been a very trying and taxing few weeks. Months, at this point."

"I'll make it happen," David said.

She stepped closer to him and clasped his hand suddenly. The look she gave him was pleading, almost desperate. "*Please* don't screw us over. *Please.*"

"I won't," he said. "I know talk is cheap and it seems like everyone out here is either evil or uncaring, but we care. And we *will* help. I promise. We'll be back once we have everything gathered. We'll be back today. Okay?"

"Okay," she said after a moment, letting go of his hand.

"I promise," David repeated, then turned and began to leave.

Ashley hurried after him. "That's some promise," she murmured.

"I don't care, we still have a fair amount of supplies. And I know Katya and April and a few others will be more than willing to help."

"And if this is some kind of a trap?" Ashley asked.

"I really don't think it is, but we're not going unarmed, obviously. And I'm sure Vanessa will be glad to go along just to keep anyone from doing anything stupid."

They hurried up out of the quarry.

CHAPTER TWO

It felt good to get back to the hospital and its people.

It had been a few weeks since he'd visited, as he'd been so busy with the day-to-day operations of running Haven. Even now, when things were going smoothly, and had been for months, there was still so much to do. Even if only to prepare for it whenever the shit went down, as it always had. The last time they'd come was with Cait for a checkup. Thankfully, all was still well with regards to their child, though he still freaked out at least a little every time anything bad happened, no matter how minor it seemed.

It was only just two weeks ago, thanks to their trip to the hospital actually, that Cait had finally agreed that she should stop taking extended trips away from Haven. Now, at most she took walks around the immediate area. He honestly felt bad about it, he could see she wanted to wander farther, go on adventures, but even she knew it was becoming too big a risk.

"Incoming!" David called as they made their way down the path that led to the hospital's front entrance. In the winter it was a lot easier to see people coming in, but ever since everything had come into full bloom, the plant life hid the path mostly from view. It was better to announce yourself to whoever was on guard.

"David," Katya replied from up above as he came into the clearing. She smiled down at him. "And Ashley. Hello you two. Is everything okay?"

"Yeah, though we're in need of assistance."

"What's up?"

"Get Donald and Janice and Vanessa and I'll tell you. It's going to require medicine and mobility. Not exactly an emergency, but not something we can really wait on, either," he explained.

"Understood. Be right there."

He and Ashley waited out front.

"God, she's *so* hot," Ashley muttered.

"Katya? Yes, she really is," David replied.

"You've slept with her, right?"

"Oh yes. Several times now. She is...fierce."

"Fiercer than me?" Ashley asked, raising an eyebrow.

"I know what answer you want to hear but I'm not gonna lie. Yeah, she is. She's crazy."

"Hmm."

The door opened a moment later and Donald, the aging surgeon who ran the hospital, appeared. He looked...better. Healthier. It probably had to do with the fact that not only was winter over, but they weren't under constant attack now and had actually been able to enjoy a few relatively problem-free months lately.

"David. Ashley. It's so good to see you," he said, shaking their hands as he welcomed them in.

"You too, Donald," David replied, looking around.

He saw Katya, sporting freshly chopped down brunette hair and an easy confidence with a submachine gun slung over her shoulder. Vanessa, in all of her eight foot blonde glory. And finally there was Janice, the only other surgeon that he knew. She reminded him of Ellie, and not just because she was a jag, but because even now, after a good six months of semi-regular interactions, she was still a bit distant. He didn't know if it was something he did or just the way she was.

"So what's the situation? Katya said something was up," Donald asked.

"We ran into a group of travelers in the quarry. They're in a bad way. I've promised them some help. And for the record, no, I didn't promise that you specifically would help them, but I was hoping you would be willing to help," he explained.

"What exactly are we talking about here?" Donald asked. "How much help?"

"Basically, I'd say, Vanessa, you, and Janice take a package of basic medical supplies over there and pretty much just check people out. They said that some people were sick, some are injured, though they didn't really specify the injuries, and they're probably malnourished. So you'd want to cover all the bases."

"We can do that," Donald said, glancing at the others. "Katya, you'll take over here. Vanessa, go get ready. Janice, help me prepare the medical supplies."

"Good. Thank you for this. I want you to go to the hunting grounds, where the thieves had set up, and wait there. They're really jumpy right now and I'm lucky they didn't shoot me. So...it'd be best if I was with you. I'll meet you at the hunting grounds, okay?"

"Sounds like a plan," Vanessa replied. "I imagine I'm going as backup?"

"Pretty much."

"All right. You go do what you need to do and we'll meet you at the designated location," Donald said.

"Again, thank you for this. It's really appreciated."

"Well, you've certainly done enough for us," he replied.

David and Ashley headed back out, hurrying to get back home to Haven.

...

"So, would I be a total bitch if I asked you to spare ten minutes for some sex?" Ashley asked as they made their way through the main entrance to Haven.

David had actually been considering that very thing. It had been over a month since he'd last been intimate with Ashley. And she was only more attractive to him than ever. He wasn't sure why but that half-shaved look was *really* appealing to him.

"Why don't you go get ready in your place? I'll let the others know what's up. They can start getting things ready. Then I'll swing by, we can fuck, then we go help them and get going on our way," he replied.

She laughed and gave him a quick kiss. "Good. Don't keep me waiting."

He looked down at her ass as she hurried off to her and Ellie's place. She'd definitely put on a bit of weight since winter, between the better eating and all the strength training exercise, and damn was it doing nice things for her figure. As she disappeared from sight, he hurried through the main gate, waving to the people on guard. They'd finally gone ahead and built an actual guard tower by the front gate, and now two people were on guard at all times. David moved through the settlement, nodding and waving to anyone he passed.

The place was getting crowded.

Really, it had *been* crowded for a while now. The new buildings had helped, but not as much as he would have liked. They had been tossing around the idea of turning the ground floor of the main office into more living quarters, but ultimately they'd turned it into a large communal dining hall and now, once a week, everyone came in and ate dinner together.

That was the one thing David had seen lacking in almost every village and settlement and town he'd passed through in his life: a sense of community. People still had privacy, inasmuch as you *could* in a place like Haven, but the result seemed to be that people cared about not just each other, but the village as a whole more. It made coming together when bad things happened easier.

Or, it would, anyway. There had been a few attacks, but nothing serious yet.

David entered the main office and headed upstairs to the second story after seeing no one was on the ground floor. He found Evie and Cait sitting at their own personal dinner table. Cait was reading and Evie was going over her schedule.

"Hey, you're back!" Cait said, looking up as he entered.

"Yep. We've got a situation," he replied, hurrying over and giving them each quick kisses.

"What?" Evie asked, a bit of anxiety slipping into her expression.

"Nothing serious, I hope. Ashley and I have found a group of people set up in the quarry. They're desperate and need help. I've agreed to deliver a basic care package of food, water, medicine, and ammo. And Janice and Donald and Vanessa have agreed to go with me and look them over, medically speaking."

"How many are we talking?" Cait asked.

"Dozens, at least. She said about forty."

"Damn," she whispered. "What are their plans?

Are they passing through or..."

"They don't even know. They've had a lot of bad luck and..." he hesitated.

"And what?" Evie pressed.

"They said they were being harassed by some group in black leather. I don't know, it doesn't sound good. They said they lost them, but..."

"But we might be looking at another concentrated effort to take us down," Cait muttered unhappily. "Fuck."

"Yeah."

"Well, if that's true, then we're going to want these people on our side. The more the merrier...provided we can trust them."

"That's what I was thinking. I was also thinking that maybe it's about high time we got my dream project off the ground and into reality," David said.

"It's too early..." Evie murmured.

"I don't think we have a choice. Unless we want them living out there in tents in the quarry for the next few months. I know we can do this."

"I guess we don't have much choice," she agreed reluctantly.

"David's right. We can make this happen," Cait said.

"What are we making happen?" They looked over as Jennifer walked into the room. Their technically-minded wraith friend, and lover, looked happier than ever. She had settled quite well into life at Haven and he was still so glad to see that.

"The plan to fix up that town in the middle of the region, by the river," David replied.

"Oh shit. Why? What happened? I thought we were a few months from trying that," she said, walking over to the table.

"Dozens of desperate people just moved into the quarry," Cait replied.

"Oh..." she nodded. "Yeah, that'd do it."

"So what do we do?" Cait asked.

"Right now, I need that care package prepared. I'll help with it after I...deal with something else. Then Ashley, Ellie, and I will meet back up with the others and bring it to them and try and see if we can hammer out a more long-term deal."

"What...other thing do you need to do?" Evie asked with a sly grin.

"Um..." He looked around at them, hesitating.

"It's Ashley, isn't it?" Cait murmured. "You need to do her, right?"

He sighed. "Yeah. We, uh, reconnected on the trip out there and back. And we want a quickie and I don't know when the next opportunity will be–"

"Go, love. We'll get started. Just don't take too long," Evie said, her grin broadening. "I know you two have been having...difficulties. If you've worked them out, then go consummate it."

"Thanks!" He kissed all three of the women and then hurried back downstairs, outside, across Haven, and between two of the cabins to the right of the main office. Behind them he found two of the newer structures they'd built. One was off farther away, tucked into the corner of the settlement. Ellie's and Ashley's place.

He actually hadn't been over all that much, not after, at first, Ellie began to get more serious with Ashley and wanted to spend more time with just her and then, after that, it became clear that there was a bit of tension between him and Ashley.

In fact, he'd only ever had sex with Ellie once in the house, to sort of christen it.

As he approached the front door, he could hear the two women talking, the door open a crack. He knocked on it.

"Come in!" Ellie said.

"That had better be David," Ashley growled. She sounded...strained, and a little out of breath.

"Yep," he said, coming in and closing the door behind him. The cabin just had two rooms, the first room being a kitchen, dining area, and living room combination, and the second one being a bedroom that contained little more than a decent-sized bed for the two women.

As he walked back there, he found Ellie standing at the foot of the bed, wearing nothing but a pair of shorts, and Ashley laying spread-eagle on her back, totally naked, her pussy glistening, her face flushed.

"I warmed her up for you," Ellie said with a smirk.

"Yeah, now hurry. I'm fucking *horny*," Ashley growled.

"All I needed to hear," David replied as he quickly began undressing.

As soon as he was stripped naked, he hopped onto the bed with her and all but dove into her. She had her legs spread wide, ready to accept him. David laid down on top of her and kissed her hard on the mouth as she reached down between them, gripped his cock, and basically pulled him inside of her. They both moaned in sexual unity as he penetrated her, slipping into her wonderfully wet, slippery vagina.

"Oh fuck I've missed this pussy," he groaned as he began fucking her, stroking smoothly into her, the pleasure already starting a wonderfully hot burn into him.

"And I've really missed your cock," she groaned.

"Ellie's tongue is great but honestly I haven't found another guy I feel like fucking yet..."

"Same, actually," Ellie said as she sat down on the bed beside them, the blue-furred jag staring intently at them.

David just groaned in response as he began to be overwhelmed by how good Ashley felt. Her pussy was *really* fucking hot and wet right now, and super tight. The way it clenched around his rigid cock and just the pure bliss of unprotected, raw sex...

"Obviously Cait's overtime demands haven't slowed you down," Ellie muttered.

"Fuck, she never lets up now," he groaned. "Evie was complaining that Cait's hogging me."

"I know, I ate her out earlier," Ellie murmured.

"Stop talking..." Ashley moaned.

David quickly lapsed into silence, broken only by his frantic grunting and moaning. They didn't have a lot of time, which was great, because it gave him an excuse for being so fucking close to busting after just a few minutes. There were all kinds of pleasures when it came to sex, all sorts of unique flavors encounters could have, and this was one he hadn't got to experience all that much: sex with someone he was intimately familiar with already, but they hadn't fucked in a good long while.

He would experience that whenever Amanda decided to open her relationship back up, and occasionally he experienced it mildly if April or Jennifer just didn't feel like fucking all week, which did happen from time to time.

Ashley was unique, though. They hadn't exactly been regular lovers, but for a while there it had been rare for them to go more than a week or so without fucking like rabbits. She was a very vigorous lover, now more than ever because of her getting into better shape. Her nice, firm tits bounced beautifully as he screwed her brains out and she was panting and moaning as they made out with a frantic passion.

"Yes, fuck this pussy! *Fuck it!*" she screamed suddenly and then she was coming and oh fucking hell yes it felt *so* good...

David cried out as he lost himself first in her orgasm, then in his own. He started to shoot his load into her sweet pussy, pumping her full of his seed in hard contractions, each one sending a pulse of mind-blowing bliss throughout his entire body. Both of them moaned and yelled and writhed together in a union of ecstasy.

And then it was over, and they spent a moment panting, embracing, staring into each other's eyes, and then they were all business.

He pulled out of her and they got up and began to clean themselves.

"I don't suppose—" Ellie began.

"I'm sorry, no," David replied. "But later, I promise. *Believe* me, I want into that pussy probably even more than you want me in there."

"Hard to believe, I want you in there a lot," Ellie murmured. "But fair enough, we have work to do." She stood and began dressing again. "Ashley brought me up to speed. So you *do* want me on this?" she asked.

"Yes," David replied. "I'd bring more but...we've already got six and one of them is a goliath so, you know."

"Yeah, don't wanna freak them out."

He nodded and finished drying off. Feeling better than ever now that he had not only blown his load but consummated his reconciliation with Ashley, a subtle tension he'd been feeling for a month now that was finally alleviated, he began dressing.

No real emergencies or disasters or insane situations had happened since he'd very nearly died dealing with the viper threat three and a half months ago.

But now it felt like that time was at an end, somehow.

Things were happening again.

...

They got the care package put together and David carried most of it. Whatever they couldn't comfortably fit into his pack, they put into Ashley's. From there, they said their farewells and headed out. It didn't take too long to make their way over across the bridge and into the hunting grounds where once he and several others had finally faced off against the thieves that had harassed them all winter. It was the first time they'd all really pulled together and shared in a decisive victory.

They found Vanessa, Donald, and Janice there with their gear, ready to go. As they headed off, making for the quarry, David reflected on how nice it was to be able to travel ever since they'd cleared out the stalker and viper nests.

Sure, large attacks like what he and Ashley had helped repel today still happened, but they were rarer, much more manageable.

Though in his heart of hearts, he was still waiting for the other shoe to drop. Waiting to find more stalker nests, or for the wildcats or rippers to begin breeding. The vipers, at least, had been completely eradicated. Not one had been seen since about two weeks after their operation. As far as he knew, they were gone from the region.

"So what do we know about them?" Vanessa asked as they made their way towards the quarry after joining up together.

"Some," David replied. "They've been traveling for a while, they're in a bad way. Some are sick, some are injured, they're running out of supplies, they might want someplace to live. There's about forty of them. They seem to be run by two women. The actual leader is named Lori and she seems reasonable but maybe a little in over her head.

"Her second in command, Val, is a lot tougher and mistrusting. She looks more experienced and older, maybe ex-military. She sort of had that same feel as some of Lima Company. And one other thing of note: they said they'd been harassed for a while by some group in black leather armor, very organized and tenacious. They say they lost them, but it's something to watch out for, I think."

"Yeah, all we need is another trumped up group of assholes who think might makes right to come storming into our fucking territory," Ashley muttered.

"We can handle them if they do," Vanessa said.

"I hope so," David replied quietly.

They came to the quarry before long and moved along it towards the far end, studying the campgrounds from afar. Everything still seemed to be there and functioning, and hopefully no other attacks had occurred in the interim.

"How do we want to do this?" Ellie murmured.

"I think we want to play it straight," David replied. "Val has a really sharp eye. Last time Ashley hung back to cover me with a rifle and she picked her out right away. I think we should handle this directly and very straightforward. I haven't got any kind of sense that they want to hurt us. So, you know, nice and easy, hands off your guns, but be ready."

"I'm always ready," Vanessa murmured.

"I think we all are at this point," Ellie agreed.

This time, as they made their approach to the encampment, the other group was a bit more prepared for their arrival. Lori was there, leading the group that came out to meet them, as was Val, sporting her scoped assault rifle and a shotgun across her back, and there were three others, two large men and a small but fierce-looking woman, each holding a gun of some kind. They seemed very wary, especially with Vanessa there.

"You brought a lot of guns," Val said as they met about a dozen meters away from the camp, just at the edge of the slope in the land that led into the quarry.

"So did you," Ellie replied.

"We've been fucked too many times recently," Val said.

"I *really* understand the feeling," David replied. "However, I would like to keep this calm and peaceful."

"So would we," Lori said with a hard stare at Val.

"I'm going to bring you the care package now," David said.

"Slowly," Val replied.

David nodded and he and Ashley got out of their backpacks. They'd put everything into a pair of smaller backpacks, so that they wouldn't have to give up their own, given a backpack could be worth more than a rifle in some situations, and being caught outside without one could be dangerous if you found yourself in a situation where you couldn't get back to your home or even a stash. They began coming over.

"That's close enough," Val said when they got about two meters away from the group. "Set it down on the ground, take everything out."

"Why?" Ashley asked.

"Just do it," Val replied.

"It's fine," David said, and Ashley sighed, but complied.

They spent the next few minutes taking all the stuff out. There was a collection of cans of food, some bottles of water, a few packages of medication, several magazines of ammo and a box of shotgun shells, and a small toolkit that Jennifer had offered up. Val walked closer and checked it over. She opened up one of the cans and sniffed the contents, some meat. She ate some and then continued checking over the supplies. Finally, she looked in the packs themselves. Apparently satisfied, she stood up. "Okay, put it all back."

"You're kind of paranoid," Ashley muttered.

"You would be too," Val replied flatly. "Even ignoring all the bad shit that's happened recently, no one offers something without wanting something in return. And if they don't, they're trying to fuck you over."

"I get that," David said, "I really do, but even you have to admit that sometimes, as rare as it is, there are people who just want to help."

She stared at him for a long moment as he finished repacking the supplies. "I guess we'll find out," she muttered. When he finished up and offered the pack to her, she reached out and gripped it, then stepped closer. She stared down at him. Her blue eyes flared. She had to be a good six and a half feet tall, and even after knowing and fucking a pair of goliaths, he was intimidated by her, though he did his best not to show it.

"If you fuck us over, I *will* end you. Do you understand me?" she asked flatly.

"Deal," David replied, because it was the only thing he could think to say.

She stared at him for a moment, then laughed unexpectedly. "I'll hold you to that." She took Ashley's pack as well and whistled sharply. The two men came over. She handed it back to them and they took it silently.

"Now, who's the doctor?" she asked.

"The middle-aged man, Donald, and the red-furred jag, Janice. They're doctors. They want to help," David replied.

"Fine. Bring them over, we'll escort them, and just them, to our wounded and sick," Val replied.

"No," David said. Val tensed. "They'll want their friend, Vanessa, the goliath, to go with them. I think that's only fair."

Val considered it silently.

"It's fine," Lori said.

Val grunted. "Okay. If she tries anything, she's dead anyway."

"Uh-huh," Vanessa replied.

"Let's...not do anything upsetting," Donald murmured as he came over with Vanessa and Janice.

"Agreed," Val said. She looked back at the two men. "Start getting those supplies passed out to people who need it." They nodded and headed back to the camp. She looked at the petite woman with the grim expression. "Xenia, take them to the wounded, then the sick. Keep an eye on them."

The woman nodded and motioned to Donald's group. They headed off.

Ellie and Lori came forward to join David, Ashley, and Val.

"So now what?" Ashley asked.

"Now we discuss the future," Lori replied.

"Yeah," Val said. "And we find out if you're *really* committed to helping us as much as you seem to want us to believe you are."

"You need something," David replied.

"We need several somethings," Val said.

"I'm afraid she's right. We're in a bad way," Lori agreed reluctantly.

"What do you need?" Ellie asked.

"If you're truly serious about helping," Lori said, "which I...*want* to believe, then what we need right now is a rescue mission. Yesterday, before we made it here, we sent a hunting party off into the woods. They didn't come back. We sent a group to investigate, and all they found was one of them dead, ripped up pretty bad.

"I think stalkers might have gotten them. We wanted to keep looking, but we were forced to move on when a group of wildcats showed up and began attacking us. We thought they were all dead. But while you were gone, one of them showed up, severely injured but still alive. There are two more, also injured, holed up in a cabin about two hour's walk from here. If you could go and rescue them, bring them back, we would be *extremely* grateful."

"We can do that," David said.

"Thank you," Lori replied.

"Is there anything else you can offer up?" Val asked. "Advice? Info?"

"Lots," David replied. "For the moment, if you head about half a mile west, you'll find some hunting grounds. Lots of wildlife there, perfect place to hunt, relatively quiet in terms of undead. You'll also find a little outpost set up there, a bunch of shacks built around a two-story building. It's shot up kind of bad but it would serve you better than some tents in a quarry."

"I'll send a scouting party to check it out," Lori said.

"Good. Let me update my friends on what's happening, then we'll go find your people."

"Here," Val said, handing him a piece of paper with a crudely drawn map on it. "That's the route the survivor says he took to get here."

"Got it." He studied it for a moment, then passed it to Ellie.

They started heading into the camp to update Donald's group.

CHAPTER THREE

"David...does it still hurt?" Ashley asked.

"What?" he replied, glancing at her. They were walking along a trail, away from the quarry, heading to the north. At the very least, according to the map, it would be a relatively straightforward journey. Geographically speaking.

They could run into anything out here, though.

"Your shoulder. Sorry. After we were finishing up, I saw your shoulder...I'd forgotten. It looks bad," she murmured.

"Oh, yeah," he said, feeling his shoulder throb briefly in response to the memory. "Sometimes it still does, but I think it's just my brain screwing with me."

He'd very nearly died at the end of the viper incident when one of them had bitten and infected him. Although he'd recovered from it, he had a really ugly scar from the bite.

"Ashley, a *little* rude," Ellie murmured.

"Oh shit...sorry," Ashley replied.

"No, it's fine." He smirked and glanced at Ellie. "*You* are actually telling someone to employ a little tact?"

"Oh fuck you," Ellie replied, rolling her eyes.

He laughed. "Later."

Her eyes sparked. "Oh right...can we–"

"Not yet," he replied. "People are in danger."

"Ugh, fine."

"Anyway, it's fine about what you asked. It *is* a pretty ugly scar."

"I'm sorry, I didn't-I wasn't thinking."

"It's not ugly," Ellie said. "It's...wicked. And we've all got scars by now."

"Don't feel bad," David said, reaching out and taking Ashley's hand. He gave it a little squeeze. "I know you didn't mean anything by it."

"I still feel bad. I *am* sorry."

"I forgive you," he replied.

"You know what, I almost never hear people do that," Ellie said after a moment.

"What? Apologize?" Ashley asked.

She laughed. "No, I still hear that. I rarely hear someone *accept* the apology. I mean, it's one thing if you don't accept the apology, like I get that. But too many people seem to think that the right answer is 'oh, you don't need to apologize'. I mean, if you really think that, accept the fucking apology. It's as much about making the other person feel better as it is about making you feel better."

"Yeah, that makes sense, actually," Ashley replied.

They walked on along the path for a ways in companionable silence after that, keeping an eye out for anything dangerous. The path this time wasn't a road but just what seemed to be a dirt path running alongside a forest.

Some grassy fields extended off to the right side for a good distance. He could see some zombies wandering around, too far off to be dangerous. For the moment, at least. They walked alongside each other, Ellie and Ashley keeping together to his right, holding hands. He had to admit, their relationship had surprised him.

Neither seemed like they wanted a relationship, and yet one had formed. And he could tell it was fairly romantic, not just sex and a shared interest in survival. He knew that it had started because despite what she liked to play at, at least in the beginning,

Ellie *did* like helping other people.

And she wanted to pass those skills along to someone, and Ashley was good. She had a natural talent at survival, and Ellie saw that, and wanted to foster it. But that didn't account for the fact that they lived together, shared a bed together almost every night.

Told one another 'I love you'.

He was very glad to see it, they both deserved happiness. Although there *was* something he'd been meaning to ask for a little while now.

"Ashley, you think it's fair if I ask you an uncomfortable question?" he asked.

"Yeah, I guess so," she replied. "Though now I'm nervous."

He laughed. "What do your parents make of this? Of you and Ellie?"

"Oh...that," she murmured. Ellie chuckled. "They are...dealing. They were apprehensive at first. They were quite convinced that you and I were an item for a while, but I had to dissuade them of that notion. Fuck, if they knew I was fucking around with you *and* Cait *and* April *and* Evie *and* Ellie...oh man, I have no idea how they'd react. I mean, my mom told me the most *scandalous* story, apparently, about how she once dated a girl when she was my age. It didn't last too long, but I mean, if she thinks *that's* shocking, she'd flip if she learned I was having orgies once a week with mostly women." She shook her head. "I think they understand that Ellie makes me happy, even if they don't fully understand it. So, you know, it's nice."

"They bug you about grandchildren though," Ellie murmured.

"I don't know why, I can't even get pregnant."

"I probably can," Ellie said. She nudged David. "Too bad you can't knock me up, hmm?"

"You'd look *so* hot pregnant," he replied.

"God, yes. If I looked half as good as Cait...no wonder you fuck her night and day."

"She's *insatiable*," he muttered.

"Yeah, I know. She fucks you, me, Ellie, Evie, April, Akila, Katya and Vanessa if they come to visit, Lara," Ashley replied.

"I'm jealous, actually," Ellie said. "Lara won't fuck anyone but you and Cait."

"She's...shy," he replied after a moment.

"Clearly," Ellie muttered. "Shy enough to let us *watch*."

"I mean...you know, she sleeps with who she wants to sleep with."

Ellie sighed. "I know, I know. It's not like I want you to try and coax her into sleeping with me if she really doesn't want to. I'm just...not used to people telling me no for sex."

"Obviously," Ashley murmured.

"Have you been out this way before, Ellie?" David asked, studying the environment some more. There didn't seem to be a whole lot around.

"Yeah, a few times," she replied. "After I found this path. I did a little expedition, took a few days to scout it out. Honestly, there's not really much of anything up here. An old barn, a cabin or two, some building that was burned down to the foundation a long time ago. Woods, a few creeks. I know the place they're talking about. We'll probably be able to make it there in an hour, since we're used to doing this and uninjured and know the way."

"Sooner the better," David replied.

They kept walking, maintaining a brisk pace.

About forty minutes later, they reached a break in the path that led into some woodlands they'd been walking alongside for about a mile now. As they began heading into the woods, finding a handful of dead zombies and a few dead stalkers along the path, they heard gunshots coming from somewhere up ahead.

"Shit," David muttered as he took off running. Ellie and Ashley broke into sprints as well and Ellie quickly outpaced them, disappearing into the foliage up ahead. He always had a tendency to forget how fast she was when she wanted to be, and how he never seemed able to keep pace with her, no matter how fit he got.

That was one of the benefits of being a jag, though.

More gunfire joined in and something shrieked wildly. Finally, David and Ashley burst through the foliage out into an overgrown clearing with an old cabin in the center of it. Ellie was firing at a pack of stalkers currently trying to get into the dilapidated structure. They joined Ellie in helping take down the monstrous things.

David took aim with his pistol and fired off his first shot. It was good, connecting with the skull of a stalker climbing up the side of the building to get in through a hole in the roof. Its head snapped to the side and it dropped to the ground with a thud. Shifting aim, he fired again and put a bullet through the mouth of a shrieking stalker as it approached the hole in the roof. It went slack and fell in through the hole.

Hopefully not onto one of the survivors.

Ashley focused fire on several more emerging from the woods to the left, and Ellie helped him put down the ones trying to rip their way into the cabin.

One was scrambling to get in through a broken window and he shot it three times in the back. Its blood splattered across the outside of the weather-worn cabin and it went slack, getting caught on the rim of broken glass. David sensed movement behind them and spun around.

He brought his pistol up just in time to shoot a stalker that had found its way to the back of them in the face. Its shriek cut off abruptly and it collapsed into a heap not far from his boots.

He emptied his pistol putting down another trio of them approaching from the right and hastily reloaded, but as Ellie shot another one that appeared on the roof, and Ashley capped two more that came out of the woods on her side, the gunfire cut off. They waited. No more stalkers, nor anything else, emerged.

"Who's out there?!" a shaky voice finally called.

"My name is David! Lori and Val sent me!" he called back.

There was no response at first, then he heard labored breathing and shifting around inside the cabin. Finally, a face appeared in one of the windows. The face was pale and dirty, with a cut across the forehead that was bleeding. The man scrutinized them for a moment, seeming to weigh the situation, then sighed softly.

"Okay, fine. We need help," he said, probably determining that they were just going to have to risk it.

"We're coming in to help," David replied. He looked at Ashley. "Stay out here, secure the perimeter."

"Got it," she replied, and set off around the back of the cabin.

He and Ellie marched over to the front entrance.

"We're coming in now, two of us," David said as he came to stand before the door. "There's a third moving around outside, watching the perimeter."

"Fine," the voice on the other side replied.

They walked inside the cabin. David took it in with a quick sweep of his gaze, finding the interior a wrecked mess and the two people inside in poor condition. One had an injured leg, another had a wound of some kind in their stomach, a bad one.

"What happened?" David asked as he hurried over, shrugging out of his pack.

"I fell last night and fucked up my leg," the man who'd been talking with them grunted. "Vincent here caught a ricochet in the gut about an hour ago when we were fending off an attack. I take it Bobby made it?"

Ellie took the medical kit David dug out of his pack, pulled it open, and dropped into a crouch by the wounded man. She immediately set to work.

"If that's the guy you sent out to track down the others, yeah, he made it. Your people made it to a quarry about an hour or so walk from here," David replied.

"An hour? Fuck, we were so close. Who are you?" he asked.

"I help run a settlement in the region. We've agreed to help your people out."

"Thank fucking God," he muttered.

"How bad is it, Ellie?" David asked.

"Not too bad," Ellie replied. "Just bleeding a lot, but it's not too bad."

The wounded man was very pale and nearly incoherent. Ellie quickly cleaned up the wound, then bandaged it as best she could.

"Sit," she said after finishing up. "Let me look at

your leg."

"Fine," he grunted, taking a seat and wincing. David got up and checked through the windows as she worked. The sooner they could get out of here, the better. Ashley was out there still, checking the perimeter, and so far nothing had shown up.

"Are either of you bitten or scratched?" David asked.

"Thank fuck, no," the man replied, grimacing as Ellie checked his leg.

"Well, I don't think it's broken, but we know someone with an x-ray machine who'll be able to check for sure," she said after a moment.

"Fucking hell, seriously? I haven't seen an x-ray machine in a decade."

"Yeah. Your group finally lucked out, we've got a lot of cool shit and we're willing to share," David said.

"You willing to give us a home?" he asked. "I could fucking go for one of those."

"Actually yeah, probably. We just need to work things out with Lori and Val."

"Lori's reasonable, Val will come around. Just don't do anything to piss her off. Then she'll come down on you like an enraged hunter," the man said.

"I got that impression," Ellie murmured as she finished re-bandaging the man's wounds. "All right, you're good to go. We need to find you some kind of walking stick or something, because one of us is going to be tied up with carrying your friend as it is, two of us don't need to be tied up."

"I'll manage," the man replied. "Thanks again for this. I honestly thought we were fucked."

"Not a problem," David said.

They started their final preparations to head back

home.

...

The trip back took over two and a half hours and was irritating, but thankfully not due to the appearance of more than a handful of stalkers stretched out over it.

David ended up volunteering to carry the injured man at first. He'd slipped into unconsciousness, but after checking over him again, Ellie seemed confident that they could move him. David had wanted to make some kind of stretcher, but there wasn't enough material around to do so. But after a lengthy walk, they had finally made it back to the quarry, where they found Val and a few others standing by the area where the camp had once been.

It was all gone now.

"Where is everyone?" David asked.

"Well, turns out you were telling the truth. We scouted the hunting grounds and the lodge and shacks, found them to be bullet-riddled but functional, and Lori and I decided to move our people there. The last group headed off with the last of our supplies about fifteen minutes ago," Val explained.

"Good to know," David replied.

"You trust us yet?" Ashley asked.

"No," Val replied simply. "But it's a good start. Come on. Lori wants to talk to you."

"All right," David said.

They took a moment to double-check the wounded, then made their way up out of the quarry and off to the hunting grounds. They didn't talk much as they made their way up into the forest, following a path that had obviously seen a lot of activity recently.

When they reached the hunting grounds, they found a frenzied activity in progress.

David took a moment to study the group. There was a different sort of atmosphere to them now, a positive change. They still seemed caught somewhere between anxious and paranoid, but there was no question that they all seemed happier, or at the very least somewhat more hopeful.

When he had initially gone into the makeshift campsite earlier, everyone had been drained and miserable and anxious. More people were smiling now as they moved their supplies into the collection of shacks gathered around the hunting lodge and some were even laughing.

Eventually, David and some of the others from Haven had come back here and moved the corpses away, scoured it for supplies, and make some basic repairs. They turned the place into something of an outpost.

Not a place that was regularly inhabited, but a place that could serve as a refuge for the night if someone ended up out this way and couldn't get home before nightfall. They equipped it with some emergency food, water, ammo, and medical supplies, and there were enough beds to support about a few dozen people.

It seemed like that had worked out pretty well.

They moved through the camp, first tracking down Vanessa, Donald, and Janice. Janice and Donald appeared to be simply checking people out at this point. Though as the other two that David and Ashley and Ellie had managed to bring back showed up, they quickly finished up their in-progress checkups and moved over to start dealing with them, following some of Val's people into the main hunting lodge.

Vanessa was standing near the edge of the camp, talking with Lori.

He, Ashley, Ellie, and Valerie approached.

"Thank you so much," Lori said. "I saw them coming in, you saved them. And this place is quite nice compared to the places we've been staying at recently."

"You're welcome," David replied. "So...now what?"

"Got another job for you," Val said. "To further determine if you're full of shit or not."

"Val! You have *no* fucking tact!" Lori groaned, giving the larger woman a push. Or trying to, anyway. She didn't move at all. David had to admit, he was curious about the relationship. They seemed so opposite, and Val seemed more like she should be the one in charge.

"I think she'll fit in pretty well," Ellie said, making David, Ashley, and Vanessa laugh.

"Yeah...badass women who talk the talk and walk the walk is kind of par for the course around Haven," David replied.

"Oh yeah? Why are you the one in charge then?" Val asked.

"If you're so badass, why aren't *you* in charge?" he replied.

"Touche," she said.

"Besides, I said I help lead. It's a joint effort, and all the others in charge are women. Ellie's not in charge, but...she played a big role in helping found Haven," David replied. Ashley cleared her throat. "And Ashley...was kind of helpful."

"Oh fuck you, you little prick," Ashley said.

"That's not what you were saying a few hours

ago," Ellie murmured.

Ashley sighed and crossed her arms.

"Okay, okay. What's this thing you want us to do?" David asked.

"Kind of similar to what we just had you do. Maybe four hour's walk back the way we came, there was a side road we came across, and I scouted it out. There was what looked like a decently intact house at the end. It looked reinforced, but abandoned. My gut says there's some nice shit in there. Unfortunately, I got chased off by a huge pack of rippers and some hunters. I propose you and I head back there and split whatever we take eighty-twenty."

"That's *quite* the split in your favor," Ellie murmured. Val shrugged, staring at them.

David considered it. He supposed it was fair. Trust was hard to come by, and at this point his group at Haven was sitting on top of a pretty healthy supply of food, water, medicine, and ammo. The past few months had been kind to them, sure, but they were also a group of unified, hardworking, diligent survivors. And Lori's group had been dumped on for the past several months, it seemed. He nodded, finally.

"Okay, yeah. I agree to this. I'll get some people to come along. Given the distance, I think we should wait until tomorrow to do it. And, if you'd be amenable to it, I'd like to invite the two of you to come and see Haven. You can see that we come from a real place, and it's full of real people, and we're actually pretty cool," David replied.

Val snorted. "It *would* help," she admitted.

"I would be okay with it," Lori said. "How far is it?"

"Maybe half an hour's walk off to the south."

They looked at Val. She seemed to be considering it. Finally, she nodded. "Yeah, all right. Let me go update Xenia on the situation and make sure everyone's still okay."

"I'll get my stuff," Lori said.

They waited by the edge of the encampment while the women got ready.

"So, what do you think?" David asked.

"I like them," Vanessa replied. "Val's a lot like Katya, for better or for worse. I think they'd make a good addition to our little neck of the woods."

"I hope so," David said, looking out over the encampment.

...

"So, what exactly is your story?" David asked as they made their way across the region, towards home. They'd made sure all was well with Vanessa, Donald, and Janice, who were going to go home after finishing their examinations of everyone.

"We've been traveling south for a while now," Lori replied. "I used to run a little township up north. I was quite good at it, I think. Then the new creatures came. And then winter came. It got harder and harder. People started leaving, listening to rumors of places where the creatures hadn't gotten to, or strongholds. I don't know what happened to them.

"Finally, three months ago, there were less than a hundred of us, and a huge surge of stalkers attacked us. We lost a few dozen people driving them off, but when it became obvious that there were even more, we decided to flee. We packed up whatever we could and began heading south, towards another settlement we traded with. But when we got there, we found that it had burned down...

"And so we kept going, and it seemed like everywhere we went, something bad had happened or the people there didn't want us or couldn't help us. We lost people. Our town originally had close to six hundred people, that camp is all that's left."

"I'm so sorry," David said.

She sighed heavily. "So am I."

"What about you?" Val asked. "How'd you end up in all this?"

He sighed. "The short version is that I wandered into the region just at the beginning of winter last year. There was a small town called River View just a bit up to the east, on the other side of the river up there. I was going to stay there for the winter, Ashley lived there, too. Then a group of assholes, thieves who robbed and harassed people all over the region, attacked. A fire got started. Undead got in. It was chaos, and the town burned halfway down, and most of the people died in the fire. I managed to make it away with another woman, a goliath named Evelyn.

"We got to a cabin in the middle of nowhere, made it our home for a little bit, found another survivor, a rep named April. Before long we found some abandoned campgrounds and decided to take them over. Ellie and another woman named Cait were pretty much survivalist nomads who lived around the region at that point, and were helping people out here and there.

"As we started fixing up the campgrounds, scrounging for supplies in abandoned buildings, we began running into people. Survivors from River View. They were sick, exhausted, desperate, starving, injured. We were in a position to help, so we did. Finally convinced a few families to move into the campgrounds. And at some point, those campgrounds became sort of like a beacon. People started talking about it, and people started showing up, and we couldn't turn them away. So it became a settlement, it became Haven. This was after we led an assault on the thieves who kept fucking with us. That's why that place you're moving into is so shot up."

"That was where they were?" Lori asked.

"Yeah. Us and several others from around the area teamed up and took them down."

"Who's all around, exactly, besides your people at Haven?" Val asked.

"To the southeast, a little past River View, is a farm that houses a few dozen people. They provide a lot of food, and we've got a deal worked out with them. They're good people. Down to the west is a large lake, and there's a settlement of a few dozen more. They fish the lake, we're good with them, too. And then there's the hospital. That's where Donald's group lives. There's about half a dozen of them. Finally, up a little past the lake, to the southwest, is Lima Company. They're all ex-military and they occupy an old building that's been pretty much turned into a fort. We, uh, aren't exactly on speaking terms at the moment."

"That...sounds dangerous," Lori murmured.

"Yeah. I mean, they're not actively hostile, we just had a bit of a falling out. We've worked together on two operations. The first was when we took on the stalker breeding grounds and–"

"I knew it!" Val snapped.

"Wait, so you have proof that the stalkers *are* breeding?" Lori asked.

"Yes. We found nests, above ground and underground in some mines. We united damn near everyone in the region to wipe them out before they got out of control."

"Fuck me, I knew it," Val muttered. "I *told* you that's where they were all coming from."

"You were right," Lori murmured.

"Yeah, it was quite the terrifying development. But we've kept it under control after wiping them out. There used to be a group of squids living in the lake, as well as a shitload of vipers. They can breed, too," David said.

"Oh great," Val growled.

"We've wiped them out, though. That was the second operation. We worked with the squids before helping them relocate somewhere safer. As far as we've been able to tell, there's no more vipers in the region."

"Well, if you're telling the truth about all this, I'm...really impressed," Val admitted after a moment of silence. "That's quite the history."

"We've been lucky, and worked our asses off to make it happen. Also...I guess I should warn you. I don't know how you feel about them, but we have a few non-traditional inhumans living among us, and I don't want either of you freaking out."

"What do you mean by that?" Lori asked.

"One of our close friends is a wraith, and another is a nymph," David replied.

"So I've come across wraiths before," Val said, "but I've *never* found a nymph living in a town. Hell, I've never even talked to one. I've seen some, but always from a distance. How in the hell did that happen?"

"Her name is Akila. She's the last surviving nymph from her clan that lived in the forests around here. She came to us to help coordinate and put an end to the stalker threat. We genuinely couldn't have done it without her help. When the dust settled and it was all over, we offered to let her stay at Haven. She tentatively agreed and discovered she liked it there."

"That's incredible," Lori said. "Is she...here? Can we meet her?"

"I'm not sure," David admitted. "She's what you might call a free spirit. Even now she still has intense wanderlust. She comes and goes all the time. She might be here."

"And you...talk with her? Spend time with her? You have...things in common?" Lori asked.

"Yeah. She's my friend. We take walks. We tell each other stories. We do...other things," he said, hesitating short of saying 'we fuck, like a lot'.

"I'm sorry, I'm not trying to be rude. I've just spent my whole life thinking that nymphs were...rather different."

"No, I get it. And they are, from what Akila tells me. Sometimes there's still some dissonance there. And I think she's, uh, unique. I think if it had been almost any of the other members of her clan who had survived, they would have left long ago and not looked back," David replied.

"Hmm."

They walked in through the front gate of Haven ten minutes later and spent the next hour moving slowly through the area, talking with a variety of people who were out and about. They talked with Amanda, and Robert, and Ashley's parents, and Lindsay. At one point he showed them their hydroponic garden, and spoke with Chloe and Lena and Jennifer, as she was over visiting.

She'd become good friends with the two women who now ran the hydroponic garden full time. After that, they ran into April making rounds and checking on people, and talked with her for a while. Lori and Val had a lot of questions, and listened to a lot of stories.

Finally, they ended up in the main office. He could smell food and figured they must be preparing dinner. Well, that'd be perfect for Lori and Val. Sharing a meal with someone typically helped endear you to them.

Or at least that was his experience.

"David," Lara said as he walked into the main dining room.

"Oh shit, David's home?!" Cait called from the kitchen. "Good! Because I expect you to fuck the living shit out of me before dinner–" She said, her voice growing closer as she walked from the kitchen to the dining room. She froze as she saw Lori and Val. "Oh, wow. Okay. You brought company." She sighed. "Sorry. My excuse, however, is that I love him, and he knocked me up, and being pregnant makes you *really* fucking horny."

Lori just cleared her throat and blushed fiercely, but Val laughed loudly. "That's fair," she replied. "You must be Cait."

"Yes. And you must be from the group David and Ashley found in the quarry." She walked over and offered her hand. "It's good to meet you."

"You too," Lori replied.

"So what's up?" Cait asked.

"I'm giving them a tour of Haven, trying to set their minds at ease and let them know we're legit. And I thought having dinner together would be nice," David replied.

"Dinner sounds nice," Lori said.

"It smells good," Val agreed.

"Well come meet the rest of us," Cait said, leading them deeper in. As they walked into the kitchen, Evie came over and gave David a kiss.

"I'm glad you're back safe, babe," she said.

"Me too," he agreed, kissing and hugging her back. "This is Evelyn. She was the goliath I mentioned in the story who helped found Haven."

"Um, good to meet you, Evelyn," Lori murmured.

"You too. I'm glad to welcome you both to Haven," Evie replied.

"And this is Lara," Cait said as Lara stood and walked over to join them. She nodded and shook hands with them.

Val studied her closely for a moment. "You must be the one that left Lima Company."

"Yep," she replied. "I see they brought you up to speed."

"More or less," Val said. "So...obviously you two are fucking," she added, looking at David and Cait.

"Val!" Lori snapped.

"And," Val continued, ignoring her, "you two seem like you're more than friends," she looked then from David to Evie. "And...I've been getting at least fuck friends vibes from all three of you," she said, then looking back to David, and then to Ashley and Ellie. "Something about the way you talk to each other and look at each other. Am I right? Also, you can tell me to fuck off, it's none of my business, and I'll take that."

Cait laughed, then looked at Evie and David. They both nodded and Evie went back to the kitchen to check on the food.

"David, Evelyn, and I are in a relationship," Cait said. "Did you meet April?" Val nodded. "She's part of the relationship, too. Ellie?" she asked.

"Love?" Ellie replied, glancing at Ashley.

"Yeah, I don't care. Just don't talk about it outside this room, please," she said, looking at Val and Lori.

"Deal," Val said, and Lori just nodded. Val seemed really interested, as did Lori, despite how much she was blushing.

"Ashley and I are a couple. I'm also extremely close with David and Cait, and Ashley and I are intimate with all four of them," Ellie said.

"Uh-huh..." Val looked at Lara. "What about you?"

She blushed and cleared her throat. "David and Cait and I are...rather close friends."

Val laughed. "And this nymph? I've heard some rumors that they're *really* horny."

"Yes," said a new voice from the doorway, "I have sex with just about everyone in this room." They all looked over. Lori jumped in surprise and he saw Val's hand drop to her gun, then relax.

"Holy shit, you're quiet," she muttered.

"Sorry," Akila said, standing nude in the doorway. She glanced down at her voluptuous body. "I didn't realize we had guests. I should go put on clothes."

"You don't have to," Val murmured. "You're really something to look at."

"Val! Oh my God!" Lori hissed, slapping her bicep.

"What? She is."

"Thank you. So are you," Akila replied.

"Glad *someone* appreciates me," Val said.

"You should grab some clothes. We're going to have them over for dinner," Cait said.

"Very well." She disappeared back towards her room.

"She's been out all night," Cait explained. "She got back while you were out and laid down for a nap. She was hunting a pack of wildcats to the north."

"She must be quite the huntress," Lori murmured.

"Oh yes. She is exceptionally skilled," David agreed.

"Damn, there is a *lot* of fucking going on here," Val said. Lori heaved a loud sigh and walked over to the dinner table, where she sat down. "I'm impressed, is all. I mean, building a community is one thing, but maintaining a web of relationships like this between such different people is...that's something else entirely. And this has been going on since winter?"

"Yep," Cait said. She laid a hand on her swollen belly and rubbed it gently. "I was the very first one David met, out in the wild. Saved his ass and then bedded him quick."

"And he knocked you up?" Val asked.

Cait laughed. "Apparently. I didn't know I could get pregnant, he didn't know he could get a girl pregnant. But it happened. I'm about six and a half months along now."

"Congratulations," Lori said.

"Thank you," Cait replied.

"Dinner's just about ready," Evie said from the kitchen.

"Perfect, I'm fucking starving," Val replied.

They began to set up the meal.

CHAPTER FOUR

Dinner went well.

They ate vegetable and rabbit stew, potatoes, and corn. They talked for almost two hours after finishing their meal, mostly just sharing stories. David was glad to see that Lori and Val seemed to be getting more comfortable with them. He also noticed that Ellie and, especially Cait, were getting fidgety and antsy, and he felt kind of bad. He'd promised Ellie sex hours and hours ago, and hadn't had a chance to deliver, and Cait was well...

Cait. Pregnant on top of being naturally horny as hell.

He imagined he was in for one hell of a threesome soon.

Which, of course, made it harder to focus.

"Man, I gotta say, you all are some of the luckiest people I've ever seen," Val said as the conversation began to wind down. The sun was beginning to set.

"Definitely," Cait agreed.

"I've seen a lot of people try interracial relationships, and a lot of people try open relationships. Interracial works more often than not, but open? Not so much. Let alone open interracial."

"What do you make of it?" Evie asked.

"I think it's fucking awesome," Val replied. She glanced at the window, then sighed. "Well, it's headed towards dark. We should really get home."

"You want an escort?" David asked.

"No, we can fend for ourselves and I can find the way back," Val replied. She and Lori stood up. "Thanks for the food."

"Yes, thank you very much for your hospitality," Lori replied. "It's been a very...uh...interesting conversation. But a good one. Val and I and a few others will have to discuss it, but I believe this could be the start of a great alliance."

"Probably," Val agreed after a moment. "You'll come by tomorrow morning for that trip?"

"Yes. I'll bring a few people," David replied.

"Excellent. See you then."

David and Evie went with them to walk them out while the others began to clean up. They got to the front gate, wished them farewell and goodnight, then headed back inside after the pair left and headed into the woods.

From there, they checked in with a few people, made sure everything was good for the night, and then headed back into the main office. David wanted to get some sleep soon, because he intended to get up early to go help Val track down that potential stash. As he came back upstairs to the dining room, however, he found Cait waiting for him.

"You. Upstairs. *Now,*" she growled.

"Yep," Ellie agreed, walking up behind Cait. "You owe us."

"Okay, okay," he replied, holding up his hands. "I'll gladly pay in full with interest."

"Good, go," Cait replied, walking over and prodding him.

He already felt a full erection stiffening against his pants. He'd had sex with noticeably-pregnant Cait dozens of times now, and every time he did it, it was still mind-blowingly hot. Cait looked *amazing* pregnant.

He'd known she would, but he didn't realize just how much it would not just turn him on, but fire him the fuck up and drive him absolutely insane with lust. Even now he was almost falling over his own feet to get upstairs with Cait and Ellie following behind him, laughing. He was deeply glad that she was as horny as she was.

He hurried into the bedroom at the top of the stairs and began stripping.

"Well, glad someone's as horny as I am," Cait said as she came in.

"Make that two someones. I had to watch him fuck my girlfriend like eight hours ago and I've had *no* relief since then," Ellie said as she closed the door.

"Sorry, there wasn't time," he replied.

"Well, there's time now."

"Lots of time," Cait murmured.

David turned to look at her as she began getting out of her clothes. Even just watching her get nude was amazing in and of itself. She got out of her shirt carefully, she did most things carefully nowadays, and revealed her large belly. She'd had to track down larger bras and as she took it off, her tits fell out and he and Ellie just stared.

They had always been big, but now they were fucking enormous.

"Here," he said, coming over and getting down on his knees, "lemme help with that."

"Thanks, babe," she replied, smiling down at him as he began unbuttoning her pants. He got them undone and pulled them and her panties down. Good fucking lord, her thighs, and her *hips*. Again, they'd always been big, but now they were just massive. Her thighs were so fucking thick, her hips so fucking big and broad.

And her ass was fantastically fat now.

"Holy fucking goddamn motherfucking shit," he

whispered as he stared at her. "You are just...the most beautiful woman I have ever seen in my life."

"Yeah," Ellie murmured.

She laughed and actually blushed a little. "Stop being ridiculous."

"No, really. Like, oh my God, Cait. Your body is just...if I was religious, I would worship you," David replied.

"You two are so crazy, you know that?" Cait replied.

"Besides, you already do worship her," Ellie replied. "Not that I blame you. Come *on,* let's wash up and get to the sex."

"Yes, fuck, please," Cait agreed.

David got up and they walked over to the washbasin. For the next moment, there was silence as they hurried to clean themselves up. As soon as they were finished, the trio rushed over to the bed and climbed into it. David helped Cait shift down, and as soon as she was on her back, he laid down beside her and pressed his lips to hers.

She moaned as they kissed. He ran his hand slowly, gently over her belly as he made out with her, and the way she shoved her tongue into his mouth spoke of great need and an almost desperate desire.

He soon slipped his hand up to one of her huge breasts and groaned as he groped it. She'd always been pretty curvy but now it was crazy. He spent a lot of time groping and sucking on her huge tits nowadays. He found himself obsessed with them. Well, about as obsessed with them as he was with her huge thighs and hips and her fat ass.

David ran his hand down her body and spent a while groping her ass, running his hand over her thighs and her hips, feeling all her smooth, pale skin.

Ellie licked at one of her breasts and began to finger her while he did this. Cait moaned loudly as their furred friend rubbed her clit.

After a few seconds she broke the kiss. "Oh fuck, I can't take it. I need cock, now," she groaned, grabbing at him. "Get inside me."

"Can I have–" Ellie groaned impatiently.

"No!" Cait cried. "I'm pulling rank. I need him for a few orgasms."

"Fine, but you have to eat me," Ellie grumbled.

"Deal. *Hurry!*" she complained as David got in between her legs.

He was kind of sad that he couldn't lay down flat on top of her anymore, he loved that position, but resting on his knees between her legs was almost as good. Her pussy was glistening and looked so goddamned inviting. David quickly slipped his cock inside of her, and they both let out loud groans as he pushed his way into her.

Since she'd gotten pregnant, she was definitely tighter.

And *so* fucking hot and wet, because she was so fucking horny all the time.

David pushed all of his rigid inches inside of her, grabbed her hips, and began fucking her. She cried out, spreading her legs wide as he stroked smoothly into her.

"Wow, this is *so* hot," Ellie whispered as she played with Cait's huge breasts.

"Oh my God that's *soooooo* good, David..." Cait groaned loudly. "I fucking needed-*oh!*" she cried out as she began to orgasm.

"God*damn!*" he moaned as he felt her vaginal muscles begin to clench around his cock and a hot spray of sex juices immediately began squirting out of her.

"Fuck, you weren't kidding," Ellie muttered.

"Don't! Stop! *Don't! Stop!*" she begged, nearly incoherent with pleasure as he fucked her orgasming vagina.

He didn't stop, and he was glad he'd built up so much endurance over the past few months, because it was hard as hell not to bust inside of her pussy already. He wanted to really bad, but he held on, continuing to fuck her, to drill that sweet, pregnant pussy as she came. She finished coming and groaned, going slack as he kept pounding her. David reached out and grabbed her huge tits, groping and massaging them as he slid smoothly in and out of her. The feeling of her bare, pregnant vagina on his cock was beyond amazing.

"Come on," she panted as he screwed her, "fuck that pussy. I want another!"

"You'll get another," he replied.

"Ooh, wait, wait. I just remembered I promised oral sex. Lemme get on my hands and knees," she said.

"Oh hell yes," both he and Ellie said at the same time.

Doggystyle with her pregnant ass in view was fucking spectacular.

She carefully shifted around as he pulled out of her, and he could read the impatience in her movements. Ellie laid down and spread her legs, and very quickly Cait was on her hands and knees with her face between Ellie's firm, blue-furred thighs.

Ellie let out a loud sound of ecstasy as Cait started eating her out, and David quickly got behind her. He took a moment to study her beautiful, huge, pale ass before slipping back inside of her.

Cait let out a loud, muffled groan of bliss, and he joined her in doing so.

Getting back into her pussy was pure paradise.

He stared at her pregnant, fat ass as he stroked into her almost like he was mesmerized. It looked almost like a caricature, but fell just shy of being ridiculous and instead was insanely sexy and erotic. She barely fit into her pants anymore, and fuck did she fill them out better than ever. David eventually grabbed her hips, her amazingly broad hips, and dug in his fingertips, gripping them tightly as he fucked her brains out. He could hear his skin slapping against hers over the two women moaning in desperate pleasure.

Ellie had an orgasm within two minutes, and she moaned loudly as she twisted and writhed, running her fingers through Cait's red hair. Cait kept pleasuring her until she was finished, just in time for her own orgasm. She let out a panting cry of pleasure as she began coming on his dick again. David groaned, hunching forward, and reached under her, grabbing her big tits as she came. It was so hard not to blow his load.

Somehow, he managed to hold on.

As soon as she was finished coming a second time, he pulled out of her.

"Okay, move your big ass," he said, patting it.

"Fine," she murmured. "But I'm not done."

"Don't worry, love."

As soon as she was out of the way, he almost dove onto Ellie, who was laying on her back, panting, recovering from her own orgasm. She cried out as he penetrated her.

"Oh yes! Fuck! Do it! *Do me!*" she cried as he began thrusting furiously into her.

"Oh fuck, Ellie!" he moaned. Fuck, her pussy was so *sweet*! It was *so* good to fuck. "I'm going to come so fucking much..."

"Lemme come first," she groaned, kissing him between moans.

"I will, I promise...oh God, this is so good..."

He drove furiously into her again and again, pounding her into the mattress, feeling her soft, hot fur against his skin as they made frantic, passionate love. He kept going until he couldn't hold out any longer and, several minutes later, she began to orgasm all over his cock.

He let out a loud groan of bliss as he triggered immediately and started pumping her full of his seed. David lost himself in the pleasured ecstasy that consumed him in waves with each spurt of his seed, each twitch of his cock, each jerk of his hips.

He could feel her writhing and shuddering against him, sharing in his bliss.

Ellie had wonderful orgasms.

As soon as they were both finished coming, he immediately pulled out and got back to Cait. Pushing her legs open, he slid back into her and she moaned loudly.

"Couldn't get enough, huh?" she asked.

"I really can't," he replied. "Your pussy has always been amazing, but this pregnant pussy of yours is just...holy fuck," he groaned.

He grabbed her huge tits and groped them as he screwed her fantastically wet, tight pussy, just going and going and going, driving into her with a furious passion until he had made her come again and he started coming once more. David cried out, panting and grunting as the ecstasy assaulted his whole body once again.

Coming inside of Cait was different now, and different than anyone else. He figured it was probably because she was pregnant thanks to him, and that as a result of that they had grown closer in a way none of the others had with either of them.

He filled her up and stared into her eyes the whole time, with her staring right back at him, her hands on the backs of his as he groped her huge breasts.

"I love you," she murmured when they were finished.

"I love you too," he replied, and slowly pulled out of her. Then he laid down between them and hugged Ellie. "And I love you, Ellie."

"Oh, I love you both so much," Ellie murmured, hugging him back, sighing contently. "You have no idea the depth of comfort that brings me."

"I think we've got something of an idea, dear," Cait replied, smiling and running a hand up and down her blue-furred arm. Then she patted David's back. "You'll need to wash up and recover, because Lara was eyeing you all night."

He yawned. "Fuck, I'm tired."

"I know. But you've got a responsibility to us, I believe," Cait said, laughing.

"Hey, I'm not complaining," he replied. "I just need ten minutes."

There was a knock at the door. "You guys done?" came Lara's voice.

"Looks like you're up," Ellie said.

...

"Oh...fuck...what's happening?" David muttered as he felt warm hands on him and the blanket shifting.

"Sex," came a familiar voice.

A voluptuous woman mounted him, and then he felt fingers wrap around his stiff erection, and then he groaned loudly as an explosion of hot pleasure hit him.

"Good morning, Akila," he moaned as she began to fuck herself with his cock.

"Good morning, David," she murmured back at him. He reached up and cupped her large breasts in his hands. "It is my turn, now."

"Apparently...oh fuck, that's such amazing pussy," he groaned, squeezing her big tits as she rode him. Her pussy felt incredible, so slick and *so* hot, a fantastic tightness around his rigid length, bathing him in a wash of pleasure.

At this point, his days starting out like this were fairly common. It wasn't like he could fuck every woman in his life every single day. Even now he didn't have that level of stamina, especially not with Cait being fucking sex-crazy.

Akila continued riding him, going faster and harder, putting her considerable thighs to good use. She was probably in the best shape of all of them and fuck did it show when she fucked him. She was incredibly athletic and vigorous and he loved running his hands over her. He slid them down from her breasts to her big, firm hips, then back around to her wonderfully padded ass, squeezing it as she fucked his brains out.

She kept going until both of them had come hard, then she smiled, kissed him, got up, and began to clean herself up.

"Am I to understand you are going on an expedition today?" she asked.

"Yeah. We're going to help Val track down some

supplies," David replied. "Why?"

"I want in," she said.

"All right. I'd welcome your help," he said.

"But first," Cait said beside him, putting a hand on his shoulder as he tried to get up, "I need morning sex."

"So do I," Evie murmured sleepily beside Cait.

"Okay, quickies though," David replied.

"We'll see," Cait said firmly as she mounted him.

. . .

An hour and a half later, he was walking up on Lori's and Val's encampment with Ellie, Akila, and Lara backing him up. All four of them were decked out and ready for a lengthy walk. As he approached the camp, he had to admit that he missed this. It had been months since he'd gone on any kind of serious expedition away from the region. The lengthy walks were dangerous, yeah, but they were also exciting and, in a sort of crazy way, fun.

"Hold up," one of the guards who was patrolling the perimeter said. He held a shotgun and shifted nervously as they came to a halt. "What do you want?"

"We need to talk to Val," David replied. "We're here to help."

He seemed to consider that for a moment, then waved someone else over. When another guard came over, he didn't take his eyes from them as he spoke to her. "Go get Val."

"On it," she replied, hurrying off.

David wondered if the man recognized him or Ellie. Probably not everyone had gotten a look at them yesterday, though while he had to admit he was probably a bit hard to remember, Ellie shouldn't be. Her blue fur was so obvious.

A moment later, Val came over, and she looked...

Quite nice, actually.

It was obvious she had a few decades on him. She might actually be twice his age. Wrinkles had gathered around her eyes and she had the look of someone who'd lived a hard life, but that didn't really detract from the air of authority and confident certainty she exuded and carried herself with.

She was wearing a tanktop and clearly no bra, as he could see her nipples and the outline of her breasts through the fabric, and they looked pretty good. And her thick thighs and broad hips filled out the cargo shorts she was wearing. A pistol and a knife hung from her belt, she had another pistol down one of her big boots, and an assault rifle slung over one shoulder.

"You all actually look pretty competent," she said as she approached.

"Wish I could say the same," Ellie replied. David glanced at her quickly, but Val simply laughed as she came to stand by them.

"Fair enough," she said. "Okay, you ready?"

"We're ready," David replied.

"Come on then. We've got a long walk ahead of us."

She turned and began heading away, back towards the quarry, and the four of them moved after her, prepared for a long journey.

...

For the first hour, they didn't say anything.

They just walked, making brisk progress past the quarry and then along the trail that David and Ellie and Ashley had followed the previous day. About the time they made it past the place where they had helped the survivors, Val broke the silence.

"So I bet you and Cait fucked like rabbits last night, right?" she asked, looking at David.

He was thrown briefly off balance, but tried not to let it show. As much as he'd gotten used to talking about sex openly, it still threw him off.

"Yeah," he replied. "We did. Why?"

"I'm just curious. I love hearing about sex. I'm a pervert. What's your favorite position?" she asked.

Ellie laughed. "Good lord, you really do have no tact."

Val shrugged. "You don't seem like you care. It's not like I say this shit to *everyone* I run into. The only one who seems uncomfortable with this conversation is Lara, and I get the feeling you're only uncomfortable because it's reflexive, not because you intentionally have a problem talking about or hearing about this stuff. Unless I'm wrong. If I'm wrong, tell me and I'll shut up."

"No...you're not wrong," Lara admitted. "I'm still...getting used to it all. David and Cait have helped me figure out some things, and that's been nice. I'm still just, uh, settling into it all. Sex is...it's always been a somewhat difficult subject for me."

"That's fair," Val replied. "It was for me for a long time, too. I hated it, at first. I've always been big and ugly and I scared all the boys when I was growing up."

"You're not ugly," Akila murmured.

She shrugged. "I appreciate it, but at this point I

don't care anymore. Either people find me attractive or they don't. Whether or not people find me attractive doesn't concern me overly much anymore. I'm fucking fifty."

"You're *fifty?*" Ellie asked.

"Yep."

"Holy shit, you've aged pretty nicely."

She laughed. "See if you feel that way after you see me naked."

"Are you saying that's a possibility?" Ellie asked.

"Sure could be. I'd like to see all of you naked. I'd like to see just about everyone naked, but I think that's true of most of us. I just admit it. Anyway, like I said, you don't really get to choose who you're turned on by, but you *do* get to choose what comes out of your mouth. So what took more time to get over was being called ugly. But at this point I don't care anymore. I just want to talk about sex with other people who want to talk about it."

David considered it for a moment. "Don't laugh, but my favorite position is missionary."

"Really?" she asked, grinning at him. "Why?"

"The intimacy, I guess."

"Okay, I get it. That's fair."

"What's yours?"

"Riding, usually. But I also *really* like it when I'm sitting on like a table and my partner's standing and ramming me. There's something so...desperate and frantic about that, and it translates well to the sex, at least for me."

"Yeah, that makes sense. What about you, Ellie?"

"It changes," she replied after a moment. "Right now I love riding. Riding tongues or riding your dick.

That fucking look you give me when I'm on top, it's like getting fucked by me is the single greatest thing that's ever happened to you."

"He gives me that look, too," Lara murmured.

"He gives all of us that look," Akila said.

"Well...you're all *really* awesome to fuck," he replied, laughing awkwardly.

"What's your favorite position?" Val asked, looking at Akila.

"What you all call 'doggystyle'," she replied. "I rather like it."

"It's pretty great," Val agreed. She looked at Lara and raised an eyebrow.

Lara cleared her throat. "I'm with David. Missionary," she murmured.

"Oh good, I was worried you might be getting bored with that," he said.

She laughed. "I'm not going to be getting bored anytime soon. You are...quite good in bed. And I spent way too long basically celibate."

"God, I know that fucking feeling," Val muttered dismally. Ellie and Akila both immediately agreed, and so did David.

"So...Val. What's the story with you and Lori?" David asked after another few minutes of silence went by.

"You want to know why I'm not running the show?" she replied.

"I mean...yeah, basically."

She laughed. "Everyone wants to know that. Some people say I do basically run the show, which isn't true. Short answer: I don't want to. Long answer: I met Lori five years ago. When I did, I was wandering. I wandered into the town that she was running. She'd just started out, basically inherited the job after the previous mayor died. I think he had a stroke or something. Lori was his assistant, and although she's actually pretty competent, he'd more or less tied her hands for the duration of the job. He didn't really want an assistant so much as someone who was a pretty face and someone who'd deal with the petty problems of the locals whenever they whined about something.

"So he left the town in a mess when he died. It didn't help that a gang of assholes happened to be passing by and started harassing them. I happened to blow through town and when I went looking for a job, I saw a bounty up on the gang.

"Winter was on approach and they promised a place to stay, food and medicine all winter to anyone who could kill the gang, or at least get them to leave. So I met with Lori, got some intel, and then wiped them out in about two days. Got a nice big shitload of supplies from their camp, and spent the winter riding high. I got to know Lori over that winter. She's a sweet girl, and she certainly has a brain, sometimes she just...lacks discipline. She's reluctant to take that last step you sometimes need to."

"How'd she convince you to stick around?" Ellie asked.

"Well, that's the thing about Lori: she's very charismatic. By the time winter was done, she'd sunk her claws into me good and deep. She became my best friend. I don't even think she meant to. I mean, she knew she needed me, and I knew that, and I was amenable to some kind of long-term deal, but neither of us quite expected to get along so well and become best friends. But we did. After that, I became her second in command and helped her whip the town into shape. We were doing pretty well, actually, until the new breeds showed up."

"I think that was true of a lot of people," David muttered grimly.

The conversation fell flat after that. Even with all the luck they'd had, all the advances they'd managed to make, it was impossible to forget the fact that the virus had jumped to the inhumans. It wasn't even necessarily that they were now facing a whole host of new and far more lethal variants of the undead, but more of the notion that it might get worse.

This happened for no apparent reason, so what was to stop something even worse from happening for no apparent reason? David wasn't sure *what* could happen, and he tried not to entertain ideas. There were enough scary things in real life to contend with.

For now, he split his attention between his surroundings and Val.

She looked pretty good. In a way, she looked better now that he knew how old she was. Fifty. Damn. She certainly looked older, middle-aged, mature, but maybe he had a skewed idea of what fifty was. Then again, he knew that some people just aged gracefully, especially if they had active lifestyles, which she clearly did. She was definitely intimidating, but that hadn't once stopped him from being into a woman.

Her hips were pretty alluring, so were her thighs, and damn did she have a filled-out ass. Nice and thick and well-padded, straining against the shorts she was wearing. He wondered if some sex might be possible. He'd really like to get a shot at taking her to bed. David kept thinking about that as they made their way along the path. As they walked on, keeping up a brisk pace, they traded a few stories, mostly sharing close encounters or, when she began asking about it, some of the details of their sex life.

The landscape didn't change all that much as they pressed on northwards. They moved through a forest for about half of it and he made mental notes of any buildings they saw. Most of them were pretty dilapidated and broken-down, but that didn't mean there might not be something useful tucked away inside of them.

Some zombies and a scattering of stalkers showed up to harass them, and he was not surprised to see that not only was Val a quick draw but an excellent shot. If they could convince the new group to join them, then Val was definitely going to be one of the new heavy hitters. She seemed like what Ellie would end up like after twenty more years of hardcore survival. Plus, well, he *really* wanted to fuck her.

And Lori, too. She was *really* damned cute.

He wondered if the two of them had ever fucked.

"We're close," Val said after about three and half hours. "Now remember, I saw rippers *and* hunters in the area, so pay really close attention to the skies, too."

"We're ready," David replied. He checked over his assault rifle one more time, and noticed the others doing the same.

"You sure look ready," Val said. "Okay, it's down that road up ahead, maybe a quarter mile deep into those woods. Let's do this."

CHAPTER FIVE

Val led the way and the five of them pressed on.

David kept a sharp eye out as they hit the road and then began heading into the woods. He could just make out the structure at the end, a two story house that did indeed appear to be in decent condition. He looked to their left and right, into the trees that surrounded them. That was one thing that sucked about leaving winter behind, one of the very few things: vegetation and foliage made everything difficult to see. It was so much easier to hide among the leaves and bushes now.

As they made their way down the simple gravel road, David immediately began to get a sense that they were being hunted. He kept scanning the environment, and noticed that Ellie seemed particularly twitchy. He heard something to his left, glanced that way, saw the barest hint of movement between the trees. Something up ahead, to the right. He snapped his gaze in that direction, caught some leaves rustling.

Val slowed her pace, they all did.

The tension continued to mount.

"I don't think we're gonna make the house," Val muttered as she slowed almost to a halt.

"I see them," Ellie said. "I count a dozen."

"Shit," Lara whispered harshly.

"Stand your ground," Val said, coming to a halt finally. "We'll kill them here and now. Form up."

They made a basic perimeter, and David glanced skywards. Still no sign of the hunters, but the threat of rippers was more than enough for him. Within seconds, there was movement all around them, the vegetation rustling as the rippers or whatever they might be shifted closer. He finally saw dark movement and caught a flash of a red eye just to his right. Swallowing, David readied himself, finger on the trigger.

The attack came then, in a burst of foliage and shrieking undead horror.

One of them rushed through the bushes to his left, shredding them in an instant, and he fired. The burst of bullets punched the dark, scaly-skinned ripper in its narrow torso and splattered the area with its dark blood. All around him, the women opened fire, their various weapons sounding off as they cut into the mob of rippers that had suddenly appeared.

Another leaped onto the path back the way they had come and began a mad dash right for him. He saw it, razor-tooth stuffed mouth open, black, jagged claws brandished, shiny and blood-stained in the afternoon sun, red eyes glowering madly. He aimed his weapon and squeezed the trigger.

A slew of red-hot lead slammed into the thing, cutting a bloody line across its deceptively thin frame and knocking it to the ground. It squirmed and shrieked until he popped another shot into its head, splattering its brains across the dirt. Two more appeared to his right and another snarled out of the bushes to his left.

He gripped the rifle more tightly, shifted aim, fired off a barrage of shots and hosed down the pair that were coming at him from the right. They went down under the hail of lead, but it depleted his magazine and the other one was still coming at him. Gritting his teeth, he waited the crucial second and a half it took for the thing to come directly into place, then he brought the butt of his assault rifle down on its skull.

There was a sharp crack and the thing shrieked loudly. Immediately following that he kicked it hard in the chest. It was disoriented but not dead as blood seeped from its cracked cranium. He yanked his pistol from its holster and snapped a round out, firing as it launched itself up and point blank putting a shot into its forehead that disintegrated its brains and scattered its skull into bits.

He jerked to the right again as another came for him, but someone fired off a shot before he could. Its head snapped to the side in a spray of gore as it went down like a felled tree.

As no others appeared, he glanced over and saw that it was Val who'd fired the shot. She looked at him and Lara. "You two are really quick," she said.

"Hey, so are we," Ellie said as she reloaded.

"Yeah, but you're a jag and they're known for their quick reflexes, and Akila is a nymph. I imagine she's got something similar. It's hard to be that fast as a human," Val replied.

"Fair enough," Ellie conceded.

"Thanks," David replied, and Lara nodded.

They all reloaded and kept their eyes scanning the immediate area.

"I guess the hunters must've fucked off," Val said as they kept walking. "Because they sure as shit would've come flying after all that."

"Thank God," David muttered.

He hated them all, but hunters did seem to be the worst of them. Except, perhaps, for giants. Those were fucking terrifying. But hunters were the only ones that could fly. Finally, they came to the house. The lawn was overgrown, the fence had once surrounded it was little more than a few iron stakes sticking out of the ground, and the car was nothing more than a rusted, skeletal heap of metal, but the house looked like it had been home to someone at some point over the past few years.

"Is anyone in there?!" Val called out. They waited. The silence played out, only broken by the slowly returning chirping and buzzing of insects and bird calls in the wake of the violent gun battle. "Guess not," she muttered. "How do you wanna do this?"

"You're asking me?" David replied. She shrugged. He sighed. "Why don't you and Akila go in the front. Lara and I will go around back. Ellie, sweep the perimeter and stand guard."

"Gee, thanks," Ellie replied.

"You've got the best senses...I guess except for Akila," he said, glancing at her.

"No, fuck you, I've got the best senses. I'm on guard duty," Ellie replied, and marched off.

Val laughed softly. "You all are an interesting bunch."

"Evidently," Akila murmured. "I'm ready if you are."

"Let's go," Val replied.

He and Lara circled around the exterior of the old house. All the windows on the first floor were boarded up, but some on the second floor were still intact. They moved around the back and found nothing waiting for them.

"I've got your back," Lara said as they approached the rear entrance.

David nodded and tried the knob. It was unlocked. He pushed the door open, pistol at ready. The door let on a dust-covered kitchen. It looked undisturbed. As he moved in and had Lara follow behind him, he heard Val and Akila coming in the front. The four of them moved slowly and carefully through the house, but the longer they were there, the more obvious it became that no one had been here for a while.

Months, at least. A fine layer of dust covered everything, and except for one instance where maybe a ripper or a stalker had gotten inside one room at some point, the place was untouched. They cleared it top to bottom, then started searching.

As he checked through drawers and in cabinets and beneath or behind furniture, David wondered who had lived here and what had driven them off. It was obvious that they'd left in a hurry, as there was a fair amount of stuff left behind. One of the cabinets was packed full of unlabeled cans. Opening a few revealed corn in one, peaches in two others, and another cabinet was full of jugs of water. Maybe they had left when it became too dangerous with all the new forms of undead around, or maybe something else completely.

Whatever had happened, it meant that David, Val, and the others had a good find on their hands. Nothing groundbreaking, but definitely more than worth the trip out there, and thankfully about enough that the five of them could haul it back without too much trouble. They brought everything they found to the kitchen, filling up a little island of cabinets and counterspace in the middle of the room. The whole process took close to an hour, and when they were done, they loaded everything up into their backpacks.

"Okay, so...that's it then?" David asked.

"Not quite. There's one more thing I want to do," Val replied.

"What's that?" he asked, glancing at her

curiously.

"I want to fuck you," she answered, leaning against the island and crossing her arms. "And I want Ellie to eat me out."

David glanced at Ellie. No one spoke for a few seconds.

"I'll take no as an answer," she added. "I just thought I'd throw that out there."

"I'll do it on two conditions," Ellie said finally. Val raised an eyebrow. "You wash up really quick and you owe me the same thing back."

"Deal," Val replied immediately. She looked at him. "David?"

"Yeah, sure," he replied.

"Awesome. I thought you'd say yes. You've been eye-fucking me all day," she said as she started undoing her pants.

"He does that with almost every woman he sees," Lara said.

"Not *all* of them," he replied as he started taking his own pants off.

Ellie passed out bottles of water, rags, and soap, and the pair of them quickly washed up. They'd been walking and moving in hot conditions for over four hours now. Not everyone minded a lot of sweat, but David still thought it was polite.

He looked at Akila. "You mind sucking me?"

"Not at all," she replied.

"I'll just have a seat," Lara murmured, grabbing a chair and placing it where she could see everyone.

Val hopped up on the island, now nude from the waist down, and Ellie got down on her knees between Val's thick, well-muscled thighs. Akila had stripped naked once they'd gotten away from the camp and put the scraps of clothing she normally wore in her pack since she preferred nudity, especially during summer.

"Any particular reason you asked me to do it?" Ellie asked as she settled into place.

"Jag tongues feel best," Val replied.

"That's what I keep hearing."

At almost the same instant Ellie touched her tongue to Val's clit and the big woman moaned in pleasure, David felt a wet warmth envelop his cock and he was forced to look down. Akila had her eyes closed as she knelt before him, her nude, curvaceous form looking fantastically beautiful as she took his dick into her mouth and began to slide her lips up and down its length. He watched her work, relishing the absolute hot, wet ecstasy of her mouth.

Val was groaning loudly and he looked over. An intense thrill of lust and desire shot through him. Val had some really excellent hips and thighs, and Ellie looked so fucking good eating pussy.

"That's it...keep going...ah fuck..." she moaned. Suddenly her entire body convulsed and her mouth opened, her eyes closed, and she gripped Ellie's head between her hands. She let out a few moans of pure bliss as she orgasmed, and as soon as she was done, her eyes snapped back open and she looked at David as she released Ellie. "I'm ready."

"Perfect," he replied, and Akila slowly pulled his cock from her mouth, smiling up at him. He looked down at her. "Thank you."

"Mmm, you're welcome," she murmured quietly. She rose smoothly and David shifted over to Val, who re-situated herself a little. She was sitting at the perfect height to get fucked. "Just so you know," she said as he got up against her, "this doesn't mean I trust you."

"Fair enough," he replied.

She laughed. "You're pretty easy, aren't you?"

"Yep. Can I come in you?" he asked.

She considered it. "Not this time."

"Okay." He glanced over. "Which one of you is willing to take a load in your mouth?"

"I'll do it," Akila replied.

"Okay, be ready. I'll try and last but..." He looked back at Val. "You're new and older and *really* hot, so I don't know how long it'll be before I go."

"Fair enough," she replied.

Ellie joined Lara, leaning against a counter with her arms crossed, watching it all with a small smirk on her face. Akila dropped to her knees beside David as he rested his cock at the entrance of Val's mature pussy and then began to slide in.

She exhaled slowly as he penetrated her. She was quite wet, and pretty pleasantly tight. And of course hot as hell. He groaned as he slid into her.

"That's it," she whispered, staring down between them.

He pushed his way in, pulled back, slid in deeper, repeated until he was all the way inside of her. Then he gripped the bottom of her tanktop and looked at her. He pulled it up slightly and raised an eyebrow. She nodded. He pulled the tanktop up, revealing her large, firm breasts. They looked pretty damned good for fifty, pleasantly sized double-ds that fit very nicely into his grasp. He began groping them as he started fucking her, stroking smoothly into her pussy. She groaned loudly and leaned back, breathing steadily, letting him fuck her.

"This is really good," she whispered.

"How are you for kissing?" he asked.

She smiled. "I like it a lot."

Leaning forward, she grabbed him and pulled him against her, kissing him deeply. He kissed her back. Her taste flooded his mouth. It was different, and strong, intense. He twisted tongues with her as he kept fucking her, going harder as he felt her articulate her body against his own, asking for more, asking for it rougher. He ended up wrapping his arms around her and driving into her furiously as they made out.

Val broke the kiss as he hit a sensitive spot, crying out and wrapping her legs around him. "Fuck yeah! God*damn* you can fuck!" she panted. "Keep going...keep going...give me that dick," she groaned loudly.

"Oh Valerie," he moaned as he buried himself in her again and again.

He'd never fucked a woman this much older than him before. Even doing Amanda wasn't like this. There was something different about Valerie and he fucking loved it. He loved fucking her mature pussy, just screwing it hard and fast, stuffing his dick into her again and again and again. The pleasure was singing through him and he was being pushed towards orgasm. He *really* wanted to come inside of her, to just pump that sweet pussy of hers with his seed, and even thinking about it just–

"Going!" he cried suddenly, pulling out and turning towards Akila.

She was ready, taking his cock smoothly into her mouth and beginning to jack him off, working him with her fingers and her lips and the pleasure was like a bomb going off.

He cried out, grabbing her head and fucking her mouth as he began to come, his hips jerking forward as he drained his cock into her. She let him, let him push his cock partway down her throat, and she swallowed, and he yelled in absolute rapture as all those hot, wet muscles tightened around his orgasming dick.

David shot his whole load into her throat and she swallowed every last drop. When he was done, he let go and she slowly pulled his cock from between her lips.

"*Damn,* that was hot," Val murmured as he leaned against the nearest counter and got his breath back.

"Thanks, Akila," he panted.

She smiled. "You're welcome, David." She rose and wiped her mouth on the back of her hand.

Val grinned over at him as she sat there, getting her breath back. "You *really* wanted to bust in my pussy, didn't you?"

"Yeah," he replied. "I really fucking did."

"I'm glad you didn't. Actually, I'm glad you didn't do it and try to claim it was an accident," Val replied.

"I don't think you can get pregnant," Ellie murmured.

Val laughed. "Obviously I can't fucking get pregnant, and I'm not too worried about sicknesses. No, it's the principle of the thing. It's because I asked, and he respected that."

"Obviously I would," David replied.

"Not everyone does." She hopped up and pulled her shirt down, then grabbed her pants and started getting dressed. "I'm beginning to see why you're so popular with the ladies, and why you've got so many of them riding you night and day."

"Why's that?" he asked.

"Well, that was a good fuck. But I already figured you were good in bed. You'd have to be through practice alone at this point. But it's because you're respectful, and you think to ask, and you actually care about the women you're fucking, even almost straight-up strangers. That's harder for guys, in my experience. Girls ask, guys do. I mean, not *always,* but you know, generally." She finished getting dressed and pulled her backpack on. "Ellie, thanks for the oral, David, thanks for the cock." She looked at Lara. "Will you show me your tits?"

"What?" she asked, sounding surprised.

Val shrugged. "I've seen everyone else here naked or been sexual with them in some way, and you're *very* attractive. I thought I'd ask."

Lara seemed to consider it, then rolled her eyes. "Fine," she said.

"You don't have to," Val replied.

"I know." David watched as she pulled up her t-shirt and the sports bra she wore beneath it, freeing her big, pale, beautiful tits.

"Hot damn, those are some nice tits," Val muttered.

"God yes, they are," David replied immediately.

"Is that enough?" she asked.

"Yeah. Thanks."

"Uh-huh."

She fixed her shirt. "Now what?" she asked.

"Now we go home, and I talk with Lori. I think we might be ready to have a real, actual discussion about the future," Val replied.

With that, she walked out of the house. David glanced at the others, who all looked back at him. There seemed to be nothing more to say on the subject, so they gathered up their belongings and followed after her.

...

They made it back to the hunting lodge about four hours later. They'd ended up breaking once for a meal about an hour back on the road. David was happy to find that everything still seemed to be safe and sound. They headed into the main lodge after Val checked in with the perimeter guards and found Lori in the process of sorting through some supplies.

"How'd it go?" she asked. She looked nervous, and David didn't blame her. The supplies she was going over looked fairly meager, and not in the best condition.

"Pretty good," Val replied, taking off her pack, setting it on the table, and beginning the process of pulling it all out.

The others joined her in doing so and they spent close to half an hour sorting through it. In the end, they did closer to a ninety-ten split, given that they needed resources as badly as they did.

"So now what?" he asked.

"Gimme a minute with Lori," Val replied.

He nodded and they headed outside. David looked around as he waited. Based on the vibe he was getting from everyone, he had the idea that Lori was right: these people wanted to settle down. He could see it in the way they were already settling into this new area. They didn't seem eager to move on. After another moment, the door opened up.

"Okay, come back in," Val said.

They stepped back inside.

"So?" Ellie asked.

"We're ready to talk about a more permanent alliance, if you are truly interested," Lori said.

"We're interested," David replied. "But

considering the amount of effort the idea I have in mind is going to take, I think we really need to be talking with everyone else. So either I can go get them or..." he hesitated, thinking of Cait. "Well, actually I'd rather you come to Haven to talk."

"I'm okay with that," Lori said.

"Yeah," Val replied.

"Okay then. Let's do this."

. . .

"So I was hoping maybe you could give us at least a little insight into this idea of yours," Val said as they crossed the bridge over the river and headed for Haven. After making sure things were all set with their people, Lori and Val had headed out with them.

"There's a small abandoned settlement further down the right," he said, pointing. "It's been abandoned for a while now, since before I showed up, because it's been too difficult to hold onto. Although I wonder how true that is, to be honest. Maybe it just got a bad reputation. Ellie? What do we actually know about it?"

"Not much," she admitted. "It's been empty for as long as I've been here. There were a few attempts of some groups to move in, but something always went wrong. Usually they just drew too much attention."

"And you want to move us in there?" Lori asked uncertainly.

"No, not precisely. I mean, yes, but I don't plan on just making some token effort to fix it up and say 'here you go!' and leave you to the wolves. But I really want to have everyone present before we get too far into it."

"Fair enough," Val replied.

As they walked on, it really struck David just how casual he had become with sex. He still *really* fucking loved it, but if this was last year or even earlier this year, he'd be uncomfortable and awkward around Val after having fucked her.

He was admittedly a little curious about any kind of friction that might arise from that, as he was kind of getting some sort of romantic or vaguely sexual vibes between her and Lori, but that could just be nothing. Maybe just his imagination, mixed with his hopes, because they'd look really hot doing it, hot and sweaty and naked together. God, just Lori alone would be wonderful to take to bed.

But if you didn't know for a fact they'd fucked, you'd have no idea that they had. Val was treating him no differently. Which was consistent with her personality, at least. He thought that she trusted him at least a bit more than before. The fact that they were willing to go back to Haven and discuss this seriously at all was a sign of that.

He entertained himself with thoughts of doing her again, and this time finishing in that wonderful mature pussy of hers as they made their way back.

Before long, they were leading the two women back into Haven and then into the main office building. It took a moment to get everyone rounded up, but finally, he found himself in a room with Evie, Cait, April, Lara, Jennifer, Akila, Ellie, Ashley, and Lori and Valerie.

"All right, so now that we're all here, what, precisely, is going on?" Evie asked.

"We're discussing making an alliance with Lori's and Valerie's people by renovating the abandoned town in the center of the region, moving them in, and also moving some of our own people there," David said. He looked at Lori and Val. "I propose we join forces and, once the town is renovated, operate it together, with an intention of it becoming a permanent settlement and, ideally, a trading post, given its position."

"That's ambitious," Lori murmured.

"We did this," David replied, raising his hands to encompass all of Haven.

"Yeah, and you took out an army of stalkers and an army of vipers, and every other asshole who's shown up to fuck with you," Val said. She crossed her arms, then looked at Lori. "I'd have to see the details, and see the town itself, but if it's all on the up and up, I'm game."

"You're really sick of wandering? I thought you'd enjoyed getting back to it," Lori said, glancing at her.

"I'm getting too old to keep doing this wandering shit," Valerie replied. "It'd be nice to settle down somewhere for good. It'd be better to have a serious hand in creating it."

"You're all in consensus about this?" Lori asked, looking at them.

"I'm game," Ellie said, and Ashley nodded.

"I'd love to help with this," Lara replied.

"As would I," Akila agreed.

"Yes," Jennifer said. "This would be quite the project."

Cait sighed and laid a hand gently against her stomach. "I won't be able to do as much as I would have a few months ago, but this sounds like a great idea."

"Yeah, it's a good chance to help more people," April agreed.

"I'm definitely behind this plan," Evie said.

They all looked back at Lori. She smiled. "Well then...yes. I think we should do this. We should start doing it as soon as possible. Though first I'll need to speak with my people, make sure they're all onboard with this, but I'm almost positive the majority of them will be. Although..." she hesitated, losing her smile somewhat. "We're all a bit bruised and battered and exhausted, so I'm admittedly not sure how much we can offer in terms of raw labor while also trying to keep ourselves alive. That is to say, you've been *very* helpful so far and the hunting grounds are already proving to be very plentiful, but it was a rather brutal experience..."

"That's perfectly fine, Lori," David said. "Take what time you need and see to your people. Their health and safety is the first priority."

"Thank you," she murmured, then cleared her throat. "I haven't...it's been far too long since we've encountered anything like kindness."

"I'm just glad we can help," Evie replied.

"I'll tell you what, why don't Lori and I get back and tend to our flock for now, and I'll come back tomorrow morning, and we can get to work on this. You can show me this town of yours," Val suggested.

"That sounds good," Lori said.

"Sounds great," David agreed.

"All right." They started to head for the door, but Val hesitated. "David...it was good working with you today."

"You too," he replied after just a second's hesitation, not sure if she was referring to the actual work they'd done or the sex they'd had.

"And you, Ellie," she added.

"Yep," Ellie replied.

Okay then, she meant the sex.

When they were gone, Evie looked at him. "You fucked her, didn't you?" she asked with a broad grin.

He chuckled. "Guilty."

"I ate her," Ellie said. "And I'm going to get some oral in return."

"Speaking of sex," April said, "David, I'm feeling it again. I want you tonight, all to myself."

"Gladly, love," David replied, making her smile.

"Which means I'll need at least one good dicking before then," Cait said.

"Gladly, love," he repeated, which made Cait laugh.

"Do you really think we can pull this off?" Ashley asked suddenly. "I mean, I know we managed to make Haven happen, but this seems a bit bigger..."

"I think so," David replied. "We've been gathering resources for months now. I mean, it'll take a while to *really* fix it up, but we should be able to get it at least livable for all of them and some of us before too long. Especially if we get a lot of people to pitch in. I know some people are itching for a bit more freedom and less-crowded living space, and they'd jump at the chance to put in the hard work to make that happen."

"Well...I hope you're right," Ashley replied finally. "I'm down for whatever."

"Good. Let's get dinner ready, I'm fucking starving," Evie said, getting up.

David stood as well and moved into the kitchen to help her.

So far, this was going really well.

CHAPTER SIX

"Knock, knock," David said as he gently pushed April's door open.

She still had her own room, preferring a little space of her own and some privacy. She'd fixed the place up and added a lot of books to her collection, as well as a whole corner now dedicated to excess medical supplies and all sorts of different kits for different situations.

"Hey, honey," she said, smiling with an easy confidence that he was still happily surprised to see. When he'd first met April, she'd been...

Well, dying.

But even after that, she had been hesitant and anxious and nervous and felt like a burden. She looked almost like a completely different person now. She was still definitely on the lean side, but she'd filled out a bit since he'd first met her. She looked happier now, too. So much happier. He could see that a lot of the general anxiety had drained from her, although it hadn't left her completely, and never would, he didn't think.

Some people just had that problem. Some days she disappeared into her room from sunup to sunset if there wasn't some kind of emergency or serious commitment. And although their sexual relationship had slowed down, he didn't feel any less close to her. There was still such a wonderful warmth there in the way she spoke to him, hugged him, greeted him, the ways in which she interacted with him.

She was laying in her bed now with a book in hand, which she set aside as he came in and closed the door behind him.

He was just wearing his boxers.

After dinner, he'd fucked Cait's brains out, then he'd fucked Evie, because she'd all but demanded it. After resting for a bit and talking with them about some of the specifics of the great task that lay ahead of them, he'd finally washed up and headed for April.

"How are you?" he asked as he crossed the room.

"Good. Sleepy. I had a full day. It was checkup day for everyone, so I had to make all my rounds. I also did a full inventory of our medical supplies after deciding I could come up with a better organization system."

"How are we?"

"Good. There's some stuff I'd like to have more of, and obviously we're not equipped to handle something truly serious like a surgery, but for the day-to-day stuff, we're doing okay. How about you? How are you doing? You've been really busy."

He nodded as he took off his boxers and she raised the blanket for him, revealing her slim, nude, scaly body. He slipped into bed next to her and felt that thrill of erotic lust and anticipatory excitement that came from getting in bed with a naked woman pass through him.

"I'm tired, too," he replied. "And I imagine I'm going to be very tired for the next few weeks. If we're going to do this, we're going to do it right, and I'm largely responsible for dragging both parties involved into this, so I need to be there, putting in the work."

She smiled at him, ran her fingers through his hair. "You're very different than when we first met," she murmured.

"Am I?"

"Yes. Or maybe different isn't quite the right word, or give the right impression. It's more that...I guess, you had these good aspects to yourself, but they were more buried and obscured by...I don't know. I don't want to say immaturity, because you weren't immature. It's more that these great things about you, your devotion and endurance and confidence and willpower have all been brought to the forefront and polished up. They're who you are now more than ever before. I remember in the beginning, you were so scared of being a leader."

"I'm still scared of that," he replied, reaching out and running a hand slowly up and down her warm, scaly arm.

"I know, but you're a lot more confident now. And I don't think you're just hiding it better."

"You're different, too."

"I feel different," she murmured. "Tell me how I'm different."

"Well, largely what you said about me. By and large the biggest change I've noticed is confidence. You're so much more confident now than ever before. You were..." he hesitated.

She laughed. "I was an anxiety-ridden ball of fear and apprehension. I was a mess," she replied. "I'm still like that sometimes, but having a stable environment and people that I actually trust and can rely on and communicate with, people that I–" she hesitated, reached out and hugged him suddenly, "people that I love, it's done quite a bit for me."

"Good," he replied, hugging her back. "I don't even have words to describe how happy I am to see you happy."

She kissed him then, and they ceased talking as they started to make out, their hands running slowly over each other's bodies. In the flickering candlelight of her bedroom, David began to pleasure her, slipping a hand between her slim thighs and beginning to massage the smooth nub of her clit. A groan escaped her and she started to kiss him more passionately.

He gradually rubbed her clit faster and harder, and he could feel her hips working with his hand, pushing against it. She broke the kiss after a minute, panting and gasping, moaning, pressing her head back into the pillow, her eyes wide as the pleasure overwhelmed her body.

"You're so good at this," she whispered, then groaned loudly. "Fuck...you know my body so well by now, David..."

"Of course I do, April," he agreed, kissing her once more. "I love you."

She moaned loudly and began to come. "I love you too!" she cried haltingly as the orgasm started a raging roll through her slim, scaly body.

He watched her as she twisted and writhed in bliss, continuing to finger her, slipping it into her wet opening now and fucking her with it. He worked her through the orgasm, and when he was finished, she took a deep breath and let it out in a contented sigh. Then she reached under her pillow and pulled out a small container of lube she kept there. She got some out and began massaging it onto his cock.

"I thought I'd ride you," she said, smiling at him. "I want to and I figured you'd appreciate it after all the walking you did today."

"Very appreciated," he agreed.

She kissed him and, as soon as she was finished rubbing his stiff cock down, she climbed onto him. He gratefully laid on his back. He *was* tired. Even with all he'd done over the past several months, all the endurance he'd built, eight hours walking around in the summer sun was still a lot. And there was only more to do tomorrow.

April finished mounting him and then began working his cock into herself. David began to lose himself in the hot, tight perfection of her pussy as she started to bounce on him. She moaned, her small breasts bouncing as they fucked.

"You made me come," she panted, "so now I'm going to make you come so fucking hard, David. I'm going to make you fill me up."

"Fuck yes..." he groaned as he felt her squeeze down there and clench tighter around his cock while also riding him faster.

April hadn't just found confidence in the social aspect of herself, she'd gotten a lot more confident in bed after some practice and trusting that they were all telling her the truth and she was pretty good at sex.

"Do you like it?" she murmured. "Does my pussy feel good?"

"Yes," he groaned loudly. "April, it's so fucking good. I fucking love it."

"Good boy," she said quietly, smiling down at him. She grabbed his hands and brought them up to her breasts. He groped her high, firm, scaly breasts, feeling their strange texture against his skin and loving it. He still had such a thing for inhuman women. He didn't want it to come across as the only reason he fucked some of his friends was because of the fact that they had fur or scales or were in some way obviously not human, and by now he felt confident that this wasn't going to be a problem, but part of him still *really* relished the strange, darkly exciting feelings having sex with a clearly not human woman gave him.

Ellie's wonderful fur, April's smooth scales, Akila's exotic allure, Evie's huge size.

And, of course, Azure's strange, alien beauty and smooth gray skin. She had visited him twice in the months that had followed their last coupling, and both times they had made passionate love, and good lord was it fucking awesome.

April began to go faster and faster, shaking the bed with their lovemaking. The pleasure spiked, blossomed inside of him, filling him with a wonderful heat, radiating out from his core. He felt like he was close to orgasm and he wanted to come inside of her so badly. He slid his hands down her body to her slim hips, gripped them tightly, and began thrusting up into her.

"Oh *David!*" she cried in shocked pleasure, reaching down and gripping his shoulders.

"That's right, April," he growled, fucking her harder, "fucking take it. Fucking *take it!*"

"Give it to me!" she moaned. "Oh fuck!"

He screwed her extremely tight rep pussy for another ten seconds until he began exploding into her. She moaned loudly as he gripped her and pulled her down hard while thrusting up, blasting his seed into her pussy, filling her up in hard spurts. She smiled at him, her face close to his now, letting him orgasm into her and hold her tightly. The pleasure blasted through him like an eruption, like a storm raging through his body, consuming his attention and his senses until it had passed and he was left in its slowly calming wake.

"Holy shit," he whispered. "You are such a good fuck, April."

She laughed and kissed him. "So are you, dear."

He hugged her and she hugged him. They stayed together like that for a while, her on top of him, him still inside of her, feeling their hearts calming, their breaths slowing, their bodies relaxing. After a while, April cleaned herself up and then they ended up in bed together. He spooned against her back, wrapping her in his arms.

"I love being held by you like this," she whispered. "I feel so safe."

"Good." He kissed the back of her head. "I love you, April."

"I love you too, David."

They fell asleep like that.

...

The next morning, Cait woke him and fucked him while April watched sleepily.

From there, he got up, washed, dried, dressed, and quickly ate breakfast. He was a little sore from yesterday, but still ready to go. The first order of business he wanted to get out of the way was to call a town meeting and let people in on the situation. He and the others went about gathering everyone that they could for the meeting. After close to twenty minutes, almost every person in Haven had come together in front of the main office.

A few were out hunting, but otherwise everyone was here.

"All right," David said once he had everyone gathered. "I've just got a few things to say. I imagine most of you know by now that we've encountered another group of people. They're travelers, and it seems that they're tired of being travelers. They seem pretty decent, and I have proposed a working relationship. They seem amenable to it. Right now, we're still feeling the situation out, but the basic idea is that we are finally going to go ahead with the plan to take over the town in the center of the region and renovate it.

"I know we've gotten kind of crowded here, and we intend for this to alleviate that particular problem as well. For the moment, some of us are going to be working with a few of their people to take a more in-depth look at the town and get an idea of exactly what we'd need to do to begin bringing it up to par and make it secure and livable. Everyone should begin thinking about if they want to remain here in Haven, or move to the new town.

"And anyone who would be willing to pitch in in basically any way, as there are going to be a ton of different jobs, should talk to Evelyn or Cait. Today some of us are going to go begin the process of assessing the settlement. We'll let you know when we've reached the point that we can start bringing others over."

He fielded a few questions relating to the project, and was about to wrap up, when something else occurred to him.

"There's one more thing," he said. "We like to keep everyone in the loop as much as possible, so I should tell you all about this. It might be nothing, but the other group reported running into a threatening force of people on the way here, men and women dressed in black leather armor who were quite dangerous. So far, all we know of them comes from what the other group told us, none of us have encountered them, and the other group says that they stopped seeing them a week ago, and think they weren't followed here. But...just keep an eye out."

He fielded a few more questions after that, with his answer largely being 'I don't know', as people wanted more intel about the mysterious group, and then everyone dispersed except for his own inner circle.

"Val will probably be here soon," he said as they gathered around him. "We should get ready. Today should be largely about scouting and assessing the settlement."

"Who's going?" Ellie asked.

"Who wants to go?" he replied.

"I do," Ellie replied.

"Same," Ashley said.

"I would like to go, actually," Jennifer said. "It's been a little while since I've been out, and I imagine you'll need my brain for this plan."

"It would be extremely appreciated," David replied.

"I will go and watch your backs," Akila said.

"I'm definitely going," Lara said.

"All right then," David replied, nodding. "Let's start getting ready for this."

...

Val showed up fifteen minutes later, and after a quick conversation, they headed off.

It was a nice day out, the sun up but with enough clouds around and a cool enough breeze that the temperature was moderate instead of scorching. They moved away from Haven until they had reached the road that ran alongside the river and then began following it to the west, towards the abandoned settlement.

David's head was buzzing with possibilities. There was a lot of work to do, to be sure, but he was almost trembling with excitement at the thought of helping build a new settlement. He'd done a lot in his life, but the process of establishing Haven, as arduous and lengthy and difficult as it had been, was the most interesting thing he had ever done. The prospect of getting to do it again, and put what he had learned to use, and on a bigger scale, only enticed him further. And now he wasn't also scrambling to survive. He had resources and people to help.

"David," Val said.

He glanced over at her. She looked great walking in the sunlight by the river, wearing a t-shirt with the sleeves ripped off and some cargo shorts, showing off her well-maintained, bulky body. "Yeah?"

"Do you wanna fuck Lori?" she asked. Before he could answer, she spoke up again. "Wait, lemme rephrase that. Obviously you want to fuck Lori, who wouldn't? Better question is: do you *intend* to fuck Lori?"

"I mean...yeah," he replied. "Certainly I'll say yes if she asks, and if we spend more time together I'd do some, uh, pursuing down that avenue."

She laughed. "Okay. Given what I know about you so far, I feel much less compelled to say this than I normally might, but I do need to say it: You hurt her, I'll hurt you a lot worse."

He glanced at Ellie, who looked away guiltily. He'd been down that road with her before when he'd started dating Cait.

"Understood," he replied.

"I'm glad. I don't think you will, though. I actually like you a lot."

"Thanks...I like you, too. What's the story with you and Lori? I mean, like, have you ever..."

"Fucked? No. I'd like to, but I'm not sure if she's into girls. I've never gotten confirmation one way or the other. Honestly, she rarely has much in the way of romantic encounters. I think she's just really shy. I mean, I know she likes sex. She's had it and she's talked about it with me before. But I don't think I've seen her with anyone, romantically or sexually, for over a year now."

"Maybe you scared everyone off," Lara murmured.

"I *had* considered that," Val admitted. "I don't want to, necessarily, but I *do* have her best interests at heart. I mean, I want her to get laid. I'm okay with even just, you know, sex and no relationship. I think it's perfectly acceptable to use someone to get off, so long as you are being honest and up front about it, and you return the favor. Shit, if anything, I'd encourage you to pursue her. She could use a good, hard fuck after all the stress she's been under."

"I'll definitely give her one if the opportunity arises," David said.

"She is *so* gorgeous," Ashley said.

"She really is," Val agreed. "She's one of the most beautiful women I've ever seen. Although, good *lord* your pregnant girlfriend Cait is something else," she muttered.

"I know, right!?" Ellie said. "She's always been hot but she's like a fucking goddess now that she's knocked up."

"Yeah..." David murmured, thinking about what she looked like naked and on her hands and knees, taking his cock from the back... "But we should focus," he said.

They were passing through the little area where he'd first encountered Amanda and her family. He could just see the edge of the settlement farther on down the road.

"I think today should be focused on three things:

securing the settlement building-by-building, scouring it for supplies, and assessing the situation in terms of what we'll need to make this work. I also think our first primary step should be *keeping* the place secure, so having a group of people stay there on a more permanent basis and getting a solid fence perimeter established around the edge of town."

"That makes sense," Val replied after considering it. "Although that's a tall order."

"Yeah. We do have some building material leftover from before, but we're definitely going to need to secure more of it...and I think I know how we can do that, actually."

"How?" Val asked.

"A while ago, we found some trailers near what I think was supposed to be a construction site at one point to the northwest of here. That's where some of the people living with us now came from. We went back and searched them at one point and managed to find some documents and a map that showed two other such sites. One was in a valley nearby, where we've already been, but another was farther away to the northwest, maybe thirty miles or so out. We always intended to go check it out," David explained.

"That's a hell of a walk, especially to haul a bunch of construction materials back," Val replied uncertainly.

"Yeah...fuck, we'd need either a shitload of people and a few days or...maybe a vehicle of some kind. A big truck." He shrugged. "Well, whatever the case, we'll figure it out when we need to. And there it is, that's the settlement."

They had gone down into a slight dip in the land and now were cresting it, and as they did, they had a decent view of the settlement. It was about thirty or so buildings spread out over an area of land to the left of the river in clusters. A main road drove through the small settlement, going right down the middle and dividing it in half, ending in a large building with the remains of a privacy fence.

It looked like a large house, standing a good three stories. David had always thought that it would serve as a great new HQ if they ever took this place over, which they were doing now. In four clusters closer to the larger house, built off of smaller roads snaking away from the main one, were much smaller houses and cabins.

The other of the settlement was a group of buildings nearer the river, a collection of stores and restaurants. Even from this distance, he could tell that it was going to be a massive amount of work to rebuild this place. Most of the windows were broken out, there were holes in a lot of the roofs and walls, he could see several zombies moving about between the buildings, easily over two dozen just in plain view right now.

"Well, that's not too bad," Val murmured as she checked it out. "It'll be a lot of work, but it can be done piecemeal. I think we could have a portion of this place secured and built back up enough to handle our people within a week, if we work hard and get lucky."

"You think so?" Ashley asked.

"Probably. Come on, let's go have a look see," she replied, and set off.

They all followed after her. David pulled his pistol from its holster as they approached the settlement. They walked along the path next to the river until they reached the intersection, then gathered at the head of the road that divided the settlement in half. He could see a few dozen zombies roaming around and few stalkers in the mix as well, prospecting for victims. David took aim. It was time for the undead to go.

He and two others opened fire at the exact same moment, and the rest of them began pulling triggers shortly after that. Every undead creature in a fifty meter radius turned towards the sound of the overlapping gunfire and began coming for them at varying levels of speed. They began to fall immediately, bullets seeking out their rotting brains and punching holes in their skulls. David popped eleven of them in a row, one after the other, his movements smooth and precise, before his pistol was spent and he quickly reloaded.

He'd had so much practice at shooting now that he almost always hit his mark. Of course, it was easier when they were just zombies. Even in their 'evolved' state, the human undead were still the easiest to take down. Stalkers, on the other hand, were quick.

Speaking of which...one of them was coming right towards him, sprinting with a ravenous madness, slightly hunched forward, reaching for him with clawed hands. He tracked it and squeezed the trigger. The first shot grazed its cheek. The second punched into its misshapen forehead and ejected its brain matter and blood out the back of its ruined skull.

The thing flopped to the ground and rolled into a tangle of loose limbs. David was already shifting aim. He shot another two zombies in the face, dropping them like rocks, and then opened fire on another stalker making for him.

It dodged and he cursed, continuing to fire, punching a round into its shoulder, its chest, its neck, then his gun was dry. He hastily reloaded as it closed in on him, running for all it was worth, desperate to rip into him and pull his guts out. At the last second he got the magazine in, brought the pistol up, and shot it twice in the head. The thing collapsed in a heap. David let out his breath shakily.

He didn't see anymore stalkers around, and all around him the others were cleaning up the opposition as it stumbled towards them with blood-smeared mouths and grasping, rigid fingers. He took aim and got back to work.

A few minutes later, the last of the zombies had been put down. In the end, close to sixty or seventy of the bastards had wandered into the main street and come at them from the offshoot roads and all the buildings, and he could *still* hear more of them hanging around. But it was a good start. He looked around the immediate area as everyone reloaded.

There was just a single building close to the river, and it was another gas station, not very large. There was maybe ten meters or so of space between the gas station and the rest of the settlement, now littered with bodies.

"How about you and I take this building," Val said, looking at David. "Everyone else get started on that long one down there," she suggested, pointing to the nearest building on the left side of the road. "I'd bet it's a motel."

"Fine by me," David said, and the others murmured in agreement. Once they were done reloading, they headed off towards the structure.

He and Val walked over to the gas station. They make a quick sweep of the exterior of the building once they got there and, after putting down a zombie that was hanging around on the opposite side of it, got inside. The place had obviously seen a lot of wear and tear, and a lot of people coming and going over the past few days. The windows were smashed, there were dirt and debris covering the floor, several of the ceiling tiles were missing, corroded by time and weather, and the shelves were barren and covered in dust.

For the first few minutes, they worked in silence, first checking out the area and making sure nothing was hiding among the nooks and crannies of the building. Once that was done and they were sure they were secure, the pair began hunting for any potential hidden resources. David had the impression Valerie had wanted to get him alone for a reason.

After a moment, she spoke up.

"So, David, level with me: why are you doing this?" she asked.

"Doing what, specifically?" he replied.

"This, this whole operation. Helping us. Committing time and resources and people. I mean, I get that you're getting something out of it, but you don't have that bullshit veneer of a smooth-talker trying to convince other people to do something without actually giving one fuck about them. You aren't like what my father called 'the politicians'. Normally people in positions of power are like that. They're either obviously cruel and self-serving, or ruthlessly efficient, or smooth-talkers who'll smile and offer with one hand while in the other holding a gun, ready and willing to blow your brains out if it suits their needs," she said.

"Well, I'll freely admit that I *am* getting something out of this. I've been wanting to settle this town for a few months now, and having the help of you and your people will make it much easier. Plus an alliance of our people helps secure our position even more so. But putting that aside, the main reason I'm doing this is...I just...like helping people," he explained with an uncertain shrug. "I've seen too much cruelty, too much unnecessary *and* necessary violence and hatred and misery.

"I've wanted to help people for as long as I can remember, but for a really long time, I was either too scared to, or just not in the right position to do so. That's changed since River View burned down and I helped establish Haven. I *can* help, and I *will* help now."

As he spoke, Val had stopped working and instead looked at him. She seemed to be studying him closely. He held her gaze calmly.

"Well," she said finally, "either you're a world-class liar, which is possible, or you're telling the truth, which is more likely, given the fact that *all* of you would have to be world-class liars, because I'm getting the same vibe from everyone: that you're all telling me the truth."

"Does that mean you trust us? Me?" he replied.

"It means I'm closer to it," she replied simply.

"Fair enough."

She laughed. "You're remarkably patient."

"Dealing with someone else having trust issues with me isn't new. I've been through this before, in a manner of speaking. And, well, it *is* fair enough. Your trust is yours to give, or not to give. I respect that," he replied.

"I think what's causing me to hesitate is how reasonable you are. It's hard to find reasonable people nowadays." She paused, considered that. "Well, maybe not *that* rare. But it's rare to find people that are reasonable *and* willing to share their resources and commit to huge projects. Let's just say, if you and your friends are the real deal, then that's very rare, and we will have been exceptionally lucky to have found you. And luck hasn't exactly been in the cards for any of us lately."

"That makes sense," he replied. "Honestly, I'm not so sure I'd really trust me either. All I can really do is, well, do things."

"That's true." She smirked. "Keep it up, and I'll let you do me again."

"That would be *extremely* appreciated," he replied.

She laughed. "You know, that's another thing. I've had guys come after me before, but it's rare I run into a guy who's like excited to fuck me. Honestly, over the past few years they've fucked me to try to get closer to Lori. Which, you know, I can't blame them. She *is* beautiful. But you're one of the rare guys who's not just into me but like *really* into me."

He shrugged. "What can I say? Tall women turn me on. Fit women turn me on. Older women turn me on. Confident women turn me on."

"So I push several of your buttons then."

"Yeah."

"Good to know."

They got back to work and finished up their investigation after another ten minutes, not managing to find anything of any real value. David planned on doing a more in-depth search for supplies once they had the place more secure farther down the line, but he doubted there was anything hidden away in the gas station. It was a prime location for passersby to quickly investigate without actually having to go into the town.

"One down," Val said as they left the building

and began to head deeper into the abandoned settlement. "Like fifty to go."

David just sighed.

It was going to be a long day.

CHAPTER SEVEN

In fact, it was a long three days.

Between taking breaks and dealing with whatever undead wandered in from the nearby forest, mostly zombies and stalkers, but there were a few rippers and wildcats in there as well, (and there did seem to be more showing up than he would have thought), they only managed to search about a third of the buildings.

They came back the second day and managed to get through about half of the remaining buildings, first having to re-secure all the structures, given they hadn't felt comfortable enough leaving people there overnight yet.

The third and final day was when they managed to finish their scouring, and this time they came back with half a dozen people from Haven, and four more of those willing and able to work from Val's group, as well as a lot of fencing material. They had made a plan: they would build a fence around the most intact cluster of houses, which was those to the west of the large house surrounded by the privacy fence.

They had enough material to wrap around the half-dozen structures, David figured. It wouldn't be a *great* fence, but it would at least be a perimeter and give them a relatively secure area to operate out of.

They spent the rest of that third day getting the fence set up. David made sure he was there in the dirt with everyone else, hauling material, digging holes, securing the perimeter, dragging bodies off. That was a big one: the bodies. They'd ended up doing a controlled burn of the corpses in a mass grave a few hundred meters from the settlement. That had been a real shit job, but it had to be done. He got to know Val and a few of the others from her group over those three days of hard work. He'd found that swapping stories helped make the time go by faster when you were doing mindless but physically taxing tasks for hours on end.

Little things came out about Val as they worked.

She'd been a soldier for five years half a lifetime ago somewhere to the south.

She had been to all three coasts of the land, and traveled thousands of miles.

She knew how to fly a helicopter, though she hadn't had the opportunity to in over twenty years at this point.

She liked sex, but she had gotten a lot pickier as she got older.

David took that particular tidbit as a compliment. Something he'd had to figure out was that all the women who had hooked up with him seemingly casually didn't necessarily treat sex equally casually. Just because they had hooked up with him within a few days or, sometimes, a few hours of meeting him didn't mean they were easy per se, not that he thought that was necessarily a bad thing, but that they were decisive.

It was an easy mistake to make, he supposed. Val was a good example of that. According to her, she hadn't been laid in quite some time. And the sexual tension was growing between them.

She spent a lot of time sweating through her tanktop and shorts, and more than once she'd said 'fuck it' and had just gone topless through some of the work.

That had been...distracting.

Pleasantly so, at least.

As the end of that final day was coming down on them, they left a group of people behind from both settlements to guard what they had established so far. David and the others headed back to Haven, and this time Val, who had before opted to just sleep at the new settlement, decided to come and spend the night with them.

She seemed more comfortable than ever with them as they got back to Haven and then made a large meal together. She laughed and talked with them with a smooth ease that he'd seen her slowly transitioning into over the past few days. It was a testament to how controlled she was that he had only picked up on that transition after several days, and even then he'd questioned it. Nothing really had changed about how she interacted with them, at least nothing obvious.

But as he paid closer attention to her, he did pick up on small, subtle things. The way she said things, the way she acted around them, even the way she moved around them. The most obvious thing was that she turned her back on them more often, whereas before he'd noted that she tended to keep as many of them as possible in line of sight when they were working together.

He didn't think it was unintentional, either.

She was consciously making these decisions as she slowly began to trust them more.

It made her all the more intimidating, in a way. Something David was learning was how much control some people had, and how little others had. Mostly it had to do with conscious intention. A lot of people did stuff out of habit or subconsciously, without really thinking about it or honestly even realizing they were doing, like a nervous tic or chewing on your fingernails.

Val didn't do any of that. She didn't pace, she didn't bounce her leg, she didn't seem to get distracted. She had an intense focus. Honestly, it was something David realized he should be striving for. He certainly had more focus than last year and he knew he was alive because of it.

But he could get a lot more focused.

And David had the idea that he was going to have to if he wanted to survive whatever else this world was prepared to throw his way. Something he wanted to do now more than ever that he had these people in his life.

They made and ate dinner, and as the night wore on, the atmosphere seemed to grow more serious.

"So," Val said, "I think it's time we discuss the next phase of the plan."

"Yeah," Evie agreed. "Where are we, specifically?"

"Well, at the moment we have about one sixth of the town fenced off successfully and roughly ten people living there now on a more permanent basis. They've got supplies and also a flare gun we managed to find. So if they fire it off, we *should* be able to see it even from here. They're all pretty reliable people from both camps. We did a decently good job of scavenging for supplies, though we didn't find much, and I want to do a much more in-depth search once we have the proper fence built," David replied.

"So what's next?" Cait asked.

"We need more construction material, a *lot* more. And a truck," David replied.

"I'm almost positive that I remember hearing the farmers have a truck in their possession. A good-sized one," Ellie said. "I was talking with one of the guards last month and they mentioned they'd found it."

"You think they'd give it up?" David asked.

Ellie shrugged. "Maybe. I mean, we've got a really solid relationship with them, but you know how Thatch is. He can get really finicky for no obvious reason over certain things. You remember how he didn't help us take out the thieves."

"Why wouldn't he help?" Val asked.

"I don't know. I always got the impression that he was dealing with something else. Maybe someone was sick or his farm had been hit once too often at that point," David replied. He considered it for a moment. "All right, Ellie and Ashley, I want you to walk down to the hospital and then the fishing village tomorrow morning. Do a checkup and ask them if either they have any supplies they'd be willing to commit to the project, or know of where any might be. Val and I will go up to talk to the farmers about the same thing and about their truck," David said.

"Sounds good to me," Ellie said.

"Anything else?" Val asked. They looked around the table, but there didn't seem to be any other things to discuss. A broad grin split her face and she leaned forward, fixing her gaze on David. "Good. Now that business is out of the way, I'd like to address pleasure. I'm ready to have sex with you again. And I'm ready to make good on my promise," she added, looking at Ellie.

"Finally," Ellie whispered.

"It'll be worth it. David?"

"Fuck yes," he replied immediately.

"Do you mind an audience?" Cait asked.

"Not at all, but I'd be *really* happy if I got to see you naked," Val replied.

She laughed. "A lot of people tell me that

nowadays. I happen to enjoy being naked more than clothed, so that's fine."

"Can we do it now?" Val asked.

"I don't see why not," David said.

"We can use our bed," Evie said.

Everyone around the table stood up and quickly began to head upstairs, as they'd already put away the remains of dinner and cleaned up. A moment later, he was nude and standing in front of the basin, washing up with Ellie and Val, who now stood completely naked for the first time.

"Good lord, you're in great shape," Cait murmured as she slowly undressed. "I already feel so fat and sluggish nowadays."

"Comes with the territory, I've heard," Val replied.

"You've never been pregnant, I take it?" Cait asked.

"No. Can't get pregnant. Even if I hadn't aged out of it, I was rendered sterile earlier in my life. But don't worry, I'm sure you'll bounce back. From what I've heard about you, you're the adventurous type."

"I sure hope so. I get a little afraid that I'll just turn into a homebody," she murmured.

"You won't," Ellie replied. "Come on, Cait. We still have to fight with you to keep you from doing stupid dangerous shit every week. You're dying to get out there and that's not going to go away. Try not to worry."

She laughed. "It's difficult."

"Yeah, it is," David murmured.

As soon as he was washed, David moved over to the bed and climbed happily into it. Val and Ellie walked over and joined him.

"Wow, that's some bed," Val muttered as she

stood at its edge, studying it. "It must take you a lot of effort to keep it clean."

Evie laughed. "Yes, it does. Given how often we fuck, we've got five sets of sheets and blankets in rotation, and a lot of washing. It's...worth it."

"Hell yes it is," Cait said as she finished getting naked.

"How many of you sleep here?"

"This is mine and Cait's and David's room, though we have at least one visitor almost every night," Evie replied. She pointed to a mattress they had since brought up. "If you spend the night, you'll have to sleep there. You're pretty big and with Cait's current status..."

"I get it," Val replied. "I'll probably end up spending the night."

"Cool."

He, Val, and Ellie ended up in bed together, getting situated, while Evie and Cait took a seat nearby to watch the event.

Before he knew it, Val grabbed David and began making out with him again. While she did that, the large woman wrapped an arm around Ellie and pulled her closer to herself, no doubt interested in feeling all that soft, warm fur against her bare skin.

She slipped her tongue into his mouth as they made out and he ran his hands across her body. She had several scars, and he found himself wanting to ask about each as his fingers trailed across them, running down the length of her body until he slipped his hand between her thick thighs.

She switched over to Ellie, kissing the blue-furred jag, and Ellie kissed her back hard as David began to pleasure Val. He rubbed her clit and she groaned into the kiss, her hips rising against his hand as he stimulated her. He kept going until she broke the kiss with Ellie.

"Okay, ride my tongue," she said.

"You got it," Ellie replied, and swiftly climbed atop her. David kept fingering her and watched closely as Val started putting her tongue to expert use. Ellie gasped and her eyes widened. She moaned loudly and leaned forward, putting her hands against the wall above the bed.

"Oh my God," she groaned. "That's-oh wow. You've had-ah!-a lot of practice."

"Uh-huh," Val replied from between her furred thighs.

David kept pleasuring her as Val kept pleasuring Ellie.

As he slipped first one finger, then two into her and began fucking her smoothly with them, she reached up and did the same to Ellie, entering her pussy from the back and slipping her fingers smoothly into Ellie's slick vagina.

"Oh *fuck!*" she cried, sounding surprised by how good it felt.

Val was beginning to writhe around beneath her and he felt like he was close to getting an orgasm out of her. In a way, he felt like they were racing: who could make their partner come first? In the end, he just barely lost to Val. Within two minutes Ellie's voice started changing pitch, her moans coming quicker and quicker together, and then she was orgasming, twisting and writhing above her as she came. And then he had Val coming, and he fucked her orgasming pussy hard and fast with his fingers, making her let out muffled shouts of bliss as she came.

As soon as they were finished, Ellie slowly got

off of her, her legs trembling. Val, panting, looked at David. "Get in me."

He responded by hopping in between her thighs. "Can I come in you this time?"

"Yes, but I want to ride when that happens," she replied.

"You got it."

He laid down on top of her and slipped smoothly into her slippery pussy. She was crazy hot and wet, and he groaned loudly as the pleasure slid over him like a wave. She was slick and so tight and her vaginal muscles constricted around his cock as he started to screw her, sliding smoothly in and out of her as he began stroking into that sweet pussy of hers.

"Oh yeah..." she moaned, spreading her legs out wide, making good use of the bed. "Oh that's just fucking perfect."

"Yes...it is..." he panted as he humped her.

The rapture from their sexual union was making a hard and fast burn into him and he again found himself marveling over how phenomenally erotic it was to be fucking this tall, mature badass woman. And this time he would get to fucking pump her full of his seed. It had kept coming back to his mind again and again ever since they'd last fucked.

They screwed frantically and furiously, raw erotic need burning through both of them, feeding off each other. Val stayed on her back for as long as she could stand it, apparently, because after about five minutes, she suddenly demanded they switch places.

"Okay," David replied, happy to let her take the reigns if she wanted to.

"Good. Hold on."

She grabbed him and rolled them both. He was still impressed with just how strong she was, she did it with such ease. As soon as he was on his back, she got up on top of him, settled comfortably into place and began to ride him.

"Ah...wow...oh my God," he whispered as she slid her slick pussy up and down his rigid length. She looked incredible and intimidating above him, grinning down at him with a fierce lust and firm confidence.

"I gotta admit," she said, "you are a joy to fuck. It's been a while since I've screwed a guy so much younger than me, and usually when it happens, it's a combination of intimidation and happiness on their part. With you it's mostly just happiness I see."

"I'm pretty fucking happy," he replied.

"I can tell. It's nice. I'm good at a lot of things, but it *is* nice to get reminded that I'm good at sex every now and then."

"You're *really* good at sex," Ellie murmured from her position beside them. She was laying on her side, watching them with a mellow gaze and small smile.

She looked quite satisfied.

"Shit...gonna come soon," he gasped.

"Good," Val replied, and started going faster. He cried out as the pleasure slammed into him, the bed shifting beneath them with the motion of their sex. David managed to last maybe another fifteen seconds before he started coming inside of Val.

And oh fucking God was it incredible.

It was like an earthquake began raging inside of him, a volcanic eruption of absolute bliss that eclipsed his entire existence. He grabbed her huge hips and thrust up with his own hips involuntarily as the first of his seed blasted out of him in a jet of perfect pleasure.

He cried out as he rapidly began filling her up, each pump of his seed a fresh wave of total ecstasy raging through his body. He lost himself in that wonderful orgasm, in her sweet, mature pussy. He became utterly engulfed in the all-out gratification that was coming inside of her after thinking about it for so long. He could feel her pushing down, forcing him all the way into her.

He came until he was dry-kicking, then slowly came back to himself.

Val was smirking down at him. "Anticipation made it better, right?" she asked.

"Yeah...is that why you didn't let me the first time?" he murmured.

"Some of the reason. The other reason was to test you, like I mentioned. You've definitely earned this over the past few days. You're a good guy." She patted his chest and got off of him, then moved over to the washbasin. "Fuck, that's a lot," she muttered as she started cleaning up.

"He tends to do that," Cait said as she got up and moved over, crawling into bed with David.

"I suppose I should get back to Ashley," Ellie said as she slowly stood up. "Thanks for the oral. That was really good."

"Glad you enjoyed it," Val replied.

"Goodnight, everyone," Ellie said as she pulled some clothes back on and headed out. They all told her goodnight and everyone began to get ready for bed. Once she was clean, Val laid down on the mattress. Cait carefully got into place beside David, as did Evie. He felt the weight of the past few days coming down on him, all the work he had done, all the work yet to do, and within a minute he was fast asleep between the two women.

...

"So, these are farmers?" Val asked.

"Yep," David replied. It was the next morning and after getting ready for the day, they'd headed out. It felt a little weird being out with just her and no one else. The others were busy with their own tasks, either out and about, or at Haven or the new place. Ellie and Ashley had headed off to talk with the other encampments.

"What are they like?" she asked.

"Good people, but guarded. A tight-knit community."

"How many?"

"Maybe twenty. I've met most of them, but every now and then I come across a new face. We have a solid deal with them: they provide us with some food and we do jobs for them. Sometimes simple stuff like help with guard duty, sometimes more complicated things, like if someone goes missing or there's a particularly dangerous monster around. So far, it's worked out well."

"Good." She paused for a few seconds. "Are you going to talk with Lima Company?"

He sighed. He'd been considering that. "No," he replied finally. "Unless someone can come up with a compelling reason, I'm not going to. I'm not normally a fan of cutting people out of things or letting bad situations fester, but...they don't seem interested in working with us anymore."

"What was the last contact you had with them?" she asked.

He thought about it. "Two and a half months or so ago. About two weeks after the incident. One of them came to visit us, though it was a rather unofficial visit."

"What's that mean?"

"It means that I hooked up with one of them at one point and she...missed me. We had sex and a meal and spent some time together. Though she warned me she probably wouldn't be back, as her superior didn't want her doing this and she'd probably get in trouble as it was. And, sure enough, that was the last time I saw her. The last time I saw any of them, up close. I've only seen them from afar since then, doing patrols or whatever it is they do now."

"Do you think they could turn violent?" she asked.

Again, he was silent for a few seconds. "I want to say no, but I just don't know. Even Lara doesn't know, and she was their second in command."

"Best guess then."

"Best guess? No. They're outnumbered by a lot. Relations are cool between us and them, and they've pissed off the fishermen. Don't know if they're talking with the farmers, or the hospital. And now you're here, and you seem like you're in deep with us at Haven, so we probably got them outnumbered two to one, maybe even three to one now. I'm not sure how many are actually still there, if they've had people leave, or if they've recruited more people. Plus, I'm not sure what they'd gain. More territory, I guess, and resources, but at what cost? No, I'm almost sure they won't turn violent," he said.

"That makes sense," she agreed after a moment. She laughed. "You're smart for someone as young as you are. I was a dumbshit at your age."

"Really?"

"Oh yeah. Risking my life all the fucking time, getting into fights with people, just doing stupid stuff all the time. It was dumb. But I managed to stay alive long enough to wise up. Took me until my like thirties, though. I'm kinda thick that way."

"Well, I'm glad you survived," he replied.

She snorted. "Yeah, me too. I didn't think I could get into a situation as good as I'm in now, especially if all this shit you're promising actually pans out."

"You think it won't?"

She shrugged. "No idea. Probably it will. You all seem pretty on the level and like you know what you're doing. But you never know what can happen."

"Yeah, that's true," he muttered.

They came to the farm not much later, and for once William Thatch was at the front gates, thus saving them the long wait while one of the gate guards took the long walk to get the man. He was talking with the gate guards, looking like he was passing the time more than anything else, and he smiled as they approached.

"David, good to see you," he said.

"And you, William. This is Valerie," David replied.

"Pleased to meet you, Valerie." He offered his hand. "I'm William."

"Pleased as well," she replied, shaking his hand.

"What brings you around my farm today?"

"Well, Valerie here comes from a group of travelers who have ended up in our region. They've had a very rough few months getting here, and they're looking to settle down. We've formed an alliance and are in the process of renovating the central town."

William let out a low whistle. "That's quite ambitious."

"Yeah, that's what everyone keeps telling me. The reason I'm here today, beyond introducing Valerie to you, is to ask a favor."

"I'm listening."

"I've heard that you have a truck. If you do, can we borrow it for a trip out to pick up some construction materials?"

William kept his face neutral, no doubt considering the situation. He looked between him and Val for a moment, then slowly nodded. "We do have a truck, and it would be good for the job. It's a flatbed, a good-sized truck meant for hauling materials, in decent condition. We've been fixing it up. I'll need to make a final inspection of it, as I know it's not ready yet, but ideally it could be by tomorrow or the day after."

"Excellent! Thank you very much. What would you like in return?" David replied.

"Two things. The first is some construction material. We've been planning on expanding our property a bit."

"If there's enough, then definitely. We admittedly don't know what's out there."

"Fair enough."

"The second thing?"

"I imagine you'll get some good trade opportunities with a location like that. If we could hammer out some kind of agreement with regards to that..."

"Yeah, definitely. That's fair," David replied. "I'd have to run it past my people at Haven and we'd also have to talk with Valerie's people, as they will have co-ownership of the new settlement. But I think we can manage something." He glanced at Val.

She nodded. "Yeah, I think that could work. I'd

have to run it past my boss, but yeah."

"Okay, great! I'll send someone around Haven as soon as we have it ready."

"Thank you so much, William, this is great," David said.

They said their goodbyes and headed away from the farm.

"That went well," Val said.

"Yeah, provided they can get the truck working. It's hard to get vehicles working nowadays. But if not we can probably help. For now, let's head back to the new settlement and see what's up," David suggested.

"Fine by me."

They began heading for the river.

...

As they came on approach to the new settlement, moving slowly down the river, David saw Jennifer making her way up it at a brisk pace. For a second, his heart jumped painfully in his chest. Had something gone wrong? But as she caught sight of him, she smiled. She looked excited. Jennifer hurried to meet with them.

"What's up?" he asked.

"We've found something fantastic!" she replied eagerly. "That tiny building at the edge of town that was locked down? I finally got into it."

"What was inside?" Val asked.

During their initial investigation, they'd found a little structure, hardly more than a shed, tucked away behind the private property at the edge of town. It had been locked down tight and he'd asked Jennifer to get inside, as curiosity was getting the better of him.

"A water purification system! It's already hooked

into the town's plumbing system! If we fix it and find a power source, a generator or solar panels or something, we can actually have running water! *Clean* water! Showers! Baths!"

"That alone makes the past hell I've gone through to get here worth it," Val said with such conviction that he didn't even have to ask if she was serious or not.

And he knew how she felt.

A working shower, a hot shower, was a godsend.

"Can you fix it?" he asked.

"I *should* be able to," Jennifer replied. "I've checked it over and made a list of the parts and tools I'll need to make it happen. But I know for a fact that we don't have some of what we need, and I don't think anyone else will."

"What about that water purification pump we found in the bunker?" he asked.

"Bunker?" Val replied.

"We found a bunker out in the woods a while ago and cut into it. That's where we got a shitload of our supplies."

"It isn't compatible," Jennifer replied.

"Oh. Well, shit," he muttered. He trusted her to know, as she really knew her tech stuff.

"But the good news is that we passed a water purification plant on the way to the new lake when we were helping Azure and her people. Do you remember it?" she asked.

"That huge scary-looking gray building?" David replied uncertainly.

"Yes. That one." He sighed. "It's the best chance to find what we need," Jennifer insisted.

"I'm up for an expedition. Honestly, I'll go through a hell of a lot for access to regular hot showers," Val said.

"Same," David admitted. He considered it. "All right, we can make this happen. The farmers need time to fix up their truck anyway. And I'm sure some of the others will be very happy to get involved in something like this."

"Come on, let's go tell them," Jennifer said, taking his hand.

He laced their fingers together and began leading her and Val back towards Haven.

CHAPTER EIGHT

They made their way back to Haven and updated the others about what they'd learned, and the new expedition up the river. David began considering how best to handle this while he waited for Ellie and Ashley to get back.

"So we're *actually* going to be able to have showers?" Evie asked as they waited.

"Ideally, yes," Jennifer replied. "I'll need to take a look at each home's plumbing, and I imagine most of it has broken down over the years, so at first we may only have a few designated areas for showering. But we can make repairs, and possibly do some expansions."

"God, that will be amazing," April murmured. "I haven't had a shower in ages."

"Same," David said.

A few moments later, Ellie came into the main office.

"Where's Ashley?" he asked.

"We swung by the new settlement when we heard gunshots," Ellie replied. "There was an attack by some stalkers. Nothing major, but enough to warrant helping out. Lara and Akila are still down there. Well, Lara is. Akila had gone out to do some hunting and thin out their numbers, as she put it. Lara said that it was the fourth attack just today. So Ashley agreed to stay and help keep an eye on things."

"Damn," David muttered, wondering if this was going to be more trouble that he'd initially anticipated. Over the course of those three days, there had been a few attacks each day. Nothing substantial, but enough to warrant caution. He refocused. "How are the others?"

"The hospital crew is fine. Excited, really. Now that we're actually making progress on the settlement, they seem open to talking about potentially moving."

"That'd be fucking fantastic," David said. "Having them right there and having Vanessa and Katya around more often to help out."

"And to fuck," Cait murmured.

He laughed. "Yeah, that too. The fishing village?"

"No news there, really. Nothing's been happening, they can't help us with regards to a truck or material, but they are interested in trade regarding the new settlement. They also asked if anyone from Val's group might be interested in coming to live down by the lake. They've got a few shacks open and now that the vipers *and* the squids are gone, there's more fish than ever."

David glanced at Val. "What do you think?"

She considered it. "Yeah, I think I could see a few of our people being into that life. Living in a shack by a lake's edge, fishing all day. I'll run it by them."

"So what did *you* find out?" Ellie asked. "Lara said you found a water machine?"

"Water purifier," Jennifer replied.

They quickly caught her up on the situation.

"Okay, cool. So who's going on this particular expedition?" she asked.

"So far myself, Val, and Jennifer," David replied.

"I'll want to go," Ellie said.

"I would, but I'm still busy running this place, getting everything in order for the eventual transition to the new settlement. Now that a few days have gone by and nothing's exploded, people are a bit more interested," Evie replied.

"I would, but I'm pregnant," Cait said with a sigh.

"I'm sorry, love," David said, walking over and putting his hands on her shoulders. He began to massage them. "I promise, as soon as you've given birth and gotten your strength back, we'll go have a nice, long adventure."

"Who will watch the kid?" she asked.

"One of her many aunts," David replied. "Or, if it comes down to it, I will, and you can go with Ellie or Lara."

"We'll figure it out," she said, then let out a contented sigh as he kept massaging her. "You're good at that...you'd better stop before long or I'm going to make you stay."

"Good point," he said. "I love you." He gave her a kiss, and then repeated that with April and Evie. Then he turned to the others. "Let's go get ready."

...

"Jennifer..." Val said, for the first time sounding hesitant.

"Yeah?" Jennifer replied, glancing over at her.

They were walking along the river now, having left Haven behind about fifteen minutes ago after getting loaded out for the journey.

"I've got a question, but I don't want to sound like a bitch," she said finally.

"You can just ask and I'll keep that in mind," Jennifer replied neutrally.

"Fair enough." She paused, seeming to consider her next words thoughtfully. "In my experience, most wraiths live alone or, at best, coexist reluctantly with some settlements, typically living at the edge of town. Now, I'm well aware that this is largely because the majority of people are at best uncomfortable around wraiths and, at worst, openly hostile towards them. But I've also come to understand that it's a two-way street.

"That wraiths have other reasons for remaining alone. Now, I understand why you're doing well in Haven. The people there are kind to you, respectful, they treat you like, well, like you should be treated. Like a person. But I'm curious to know if there's anything on your end that drew you there in the first place."

"That's a fair question," Jennifer replied. "And well put. And I'm not mad. What initially drew me in–" She hesitated, glancing at David.

Val followed her gaze and laughed. "Wow, David, is there anyone in Haven you *aren't* fucking?" she asked.

"Yes!" he replied. "I'm *not* fucking most of the women in the settlement, for your information, Valerie."

She laughed again. "Uh-huh. How about *have* fucked?" He sighed. "I thought so." She looked at Jennifer. "Continue."

"I used to be a lot more of a social person, before I got turned. That fell away over the years, and I ended up living alone in a house in the region. For a while, my only friend was Ellie, and I was a little distant with her. Eventually, she brought me David and Cait. And David...enchanted me."

"He *is* a bit of an enchanter," Ellie said, grinning. David sighed again.

"After we, uh, connected, I began to spend more time around people. Mainly the people at the hospital at first, as they needed my help, and they were very kind to me, very friendly, and it made me realize how much I desperately missed being around people. People who were comfortable around me, people who liked me, people who acknowledged me.

"And because of that, I ended up in Haven, and it's like...like I'm not half-undead anymore." She laughed, her voice a little choked. "If I could still cry, I would be right now, honestly. David and Cait and Ellie and everyone there have been so kind to me, they've completely changed my life."

"I'm glad we could," Ellie replied.

"You deserve it," David said, reaching out and slipping an arm around her waist. She smiled wider as she stepped closer to him.

"The sex *did* help though, I'll admit," she murmured.

"It seems to," Val said. "Well that's awesome. I like hearing about stuff like this. It's too rare to hear about good shit happening or even nice stuff. Like, you know, just outright nice stuff. Too many stories I hear that people say are good are 'and then I got revenge on those fuckers by blowing their heads off', and that's...that can be satisfying, I'll admit, but it's still miserable. But your group seems to just be doing outright good shit. And I appreciate that. I know Lori does."

"Well, we like doing it," David replied. "It's definitely changed the course of my life more than any other thing has."

"You know, it might be a little hard to believe, but David used to look, and be, totally different last year," Ellie said.

"Really?" Val asked.

"Yeah. I'd say he's put on like fifteen pounds of

muscle. That's the biggest difference. But I'd say he's aged like five or maybe even ten years."

"What, seriously?" David asked.

"Yeah, but like in a good way. When I first met you, you still looked like a teenager. Now you look like, well, a man. A grownup."

"Gee, thanks," he replied.

"It's a compliment!"

He began to respond, then hesitated as something occurred to him. "Why did you lay me that first time?" he asked.

"What?" She seemed almost startled by the question.

"The first time we had sex, why did you do it? Especially if I seemed so young to you."

"I mean, I told you already: I was horny, you seemed like a safe bet."

"There wasn't more to it?"

She shrugged uncomfortably. "I don't know. I was...lonely. And there was something about you, I guess. I mean, I was right. You're a great guy."

"All right. I didn't mean to embarrass you, I guess I was just curious after hearing that."

They kept on walking, keeping an eye out for undead. David found himself enjoying the walk. The sky was overcast, threatening rain at some point, but for now it just meant no sun beating directly down on them and a cool breeze whispering through the trees and over the fields.

The river streamed slowly by them, providing a pleasant background of white noise. Though as nice as he found the walk and the company, he wasn't exactly looking forward to visiting the site they were heading for. When they'd passed it on the initial trip, the large, imposing structure had given him a feeling of ominous dread.

Maybe there would be nothing inside, but he doubted it.

...

"Okay, I can see what you mean about this place," Val murmured as they came to a halt.

The four of them now stood at the head of an old asphalt road. Cracks ran along it and weeds grew up through them. A trio of skeletal vehicles sat along that stretch of road. A large iron fence surrounded the property and it was still mostly intact. It had spikes along the top and there were several undead stuck on them. Stalkers mostly, but a few wildcats, too. A few still moved feebly. And then there was the structure itself.

It was a large, ominous gray building. The front was three stories tall, with large metal cylinders peeking over the roof from behind it. Most of the windows had been broken out over the past several decades, and the front doors were missing. About fifty meters away, David could see the entrance, just a dark gap in the pitted gray concrete.

Almost like a mouth. Like it was waiting to swallow them whole.

"Well," Val said, glancing up once at the overcast skies, which had darkened considerably since they'd set out on this walk, "let's get this over with."

"Yeah," David replied. He made himself start walking forward. He could handle this, they were all good at survival, well-armed, ready for anything.

He hoped.

They moved past the remains of the vehicles,

their weapons drawn. David had opted for a submachine gun, a nice little compact thing that took 9mm bullets and held thirty round magazines. He'd cleaned and prepared it not all that long ago, and had a dozen magazines in his pockets ready to go for it. His pistol also sat on his hip, ready for action just in case.

And his combat knife. At this point, he never went outside of Haven without at least the pistol and the knife. They checked each vehicle as they passed it out of habit, but none held anything of any real value. Given the scarcity of resources, and the potential to make a massive find in a seemingly ordinary spot, people had made a habit of searching just about everywhere.

David checked the others. Val looked as rock solid as ever, confident and sure, despite her previous statement. Although he had to wonder if she was even capable of doing anything but projecting an aura of confidence after doing stuff like this for so long. Ellie looked much the same, although he noticed a change in her. It was something that had happened over the past few months. When she'd come out of that nearly comatose state after returning to Haven and being infected by a stalker, she had been different.

He'd initially passed it off as a near-death experience, but it had persisted. She had lost something, and he thought it was something worth losing. Her cold detachment was largely gone, and her confidence had changed from something cocky and smug to something stoic and sure. Well, maybe not entirely, she still had that cavalier attitude every now and then, and honestly, he was glad she hadn't lost it completely.

Now it was more of a joke than a belief that she

was superior to those around her. Before, he had the impression that you had to fight tooth and nail to gain Ellie's respect, and even at best she would call you ally, perhaps friend, but nothing more serious.

She was so different now, and he was deeply grateful for the change. She was happier now, happier than he'd ever seen her before.

And then there was Jennifer. She was more confident than he'd ever seen her by now, in seemingly all fronts of her life. Socially and sexually, at a workbench and out in the field. She'd trained with them and now she was an excellent shot with surprisingly quick reflexes for a wraith. Months ago she would have been worried or anxious to go on a mission like this, but all he saw was firm certainty on her face as she scanned the area.

Honestly, it made him feel kind of anxious. Everyone else seemed so confident, and here he was scared of a building. Well, what it held, but he certainly didn't feel as confident as he was trying to appear. David forced himself to relax and focus. Why wouldn't he be confident? How much had he endured over the past six months? How many crazy things had he done? How many insane situations had he walked into and out of? He could do this.

He was *going* to do this.

And then he was going to do whatever else it took to secure that new settlement, cement his alliance with Lori's and Val's group, and protect those who mattered to him.

He had to admit, he felt a bit better as they approached the opening.

"Flashlights," he said as they stepped up to the opening.

One of the reasons he liked the SMG: it had a

small but powerful light built into the muzzle. He flicked it on, and Val and Jennifer did the same. Val had a shotgun with a flashlight attached manually to the barrel and Jennifer had a pistol that she'd custom-rigged (a bit more professionally) the same way. Ellie was the only one without her own light source, but she had better vision as it was. He and Val stepped up to the threshold of the large structure.

David slowly passed his light over the interior, scouring it with his gaze for hints or clues of anything threatening that might lurk within. For once, the huge warehouse-sized building was actually divided into floors, instead of having one huge, open area. The ceiling was ten feet overhead. They had come to what might once have been a receiving area for personnel, though now all that was left was the remains of a big desk. There was a door to either side of them. He saw dirty footprints all across the torn-up carpet.

Some had shoes, some didn't, and obviously belonged to wildcats.

"We might have wildcats in here," he muttered, pointing.

"I'm ready for the fuckers," Val replied.

"How do we want to do this?" Ellie asked.

"Split up?" Val suggested.

"Might be a good idea," Ellie said.

David sighed. "Yeah, I guess we can cover more ground that way. All right, Ellie, with me. We'll go right. Val and Jennifer, take the left. We meet back here when we're done."

The others nodded and Val and Jennifer set off to the left, Val in the lead. David and Ellie moved off to the right. For the first few moments, neither spoke as they slipped through the open doorway there and came into a hallway that immediately went away to the left. The floor was pitted, time-chewed concrete, the walls bland metal in similar condition.

Overhead, dead lights were bolted to the ceiling every few feet, most of the bulbs shattered or missing. David counted five doors in the corridor with them. Three in the right wall, one in the left, farther down, and one at the end, where the corridor dead-ended.

They checked the nearest door first and found a room with a tiled floor, covered in grime and old blood and dirt. Rows of lockers covered most of the walls, some missing their doors, others still sealed. They'd definitely have to come back and check those. He'd found some really cool shit hidden away in lockers over the years. They moved to the only other door in the room, which led to a bathroom. Ellie stood watch while David checked the stalls. All he found was a dead body, long decayed, sitting on one of the toilets.

He shut that door and they moved on, coming back out into the corridor through the bathroom door and then moving down to the third and final entrance in the right wall. As David reached for the handle, he hesitated, hearing something overhead.

A dull thump that was so faint he wasn't sure he'd heard anything at first. But from the way Ellie tensed up, he knew there had been a sound. They both glanced up and then at each other. After a second, they agreed that the best course of action was to keep searching with a wary eye.

The third door on the right led to a storeroom that had been mostly picked clean. Nothing but bare metal shelves with the occasional dust-covered item left behind. They checked the niches and potential hiding spots, then moved on.

The door at the end of the corridor was locked,

firmly. It had a padlock holding the door closed tightly and the door itself was pretty solid steel.

"Where do you think this goes?" Ellie asked.

"Basement," David replied, pointing to a little faded yellow sign that had an image of stairs and an arrow hovering over it pointing down.

"Probably where we need to get," she muttered.

"Yeah. We'll find a way in. Come on."

As they stepped into the final room, passing through the door in the left wall, David's heart kicked painfully in his chest as he saw movement and another flashlight directly across from him. But he relaxed as he realized it was just Val and Jennifer.

"Fancy seeing you here," Val said. "You find anything?"

"Locked door to the basement," David replied. "Not a lot else. You?"

"A break room, a few storage rooms, an office, a stairway leading up. Just a few corpses, maybe places for useful supplies, nothing else. Heard some activity upstairs, though."

"Same," David replied.

"We'll almost certainly need to getf into the basement," Jennifer said. "I imagine that's where the guts of the equipment is, and, more specifically, the parts I need."

"It's padlocked and it's pretty solid. Hopefully we can find a key," Ellie replied.

"Or some bolt-cutters," Val said.

"Let's search this room, then head up and see what's waiting for us," David said.

The room they had come into was a galley, a place to gather and eat for the people who had once worked here, before the end of the world. They performed a quick search, their flashlight beams shifting about in the room. The only windows were a row high in the wall at the back of the room, behind the serving line, and they were mostly covered in filth.

David slipped back into the kitchen area, shining his light beneath the serving line and among the large ovens and refrigerators. He found a dead body, a long-dead stalker, near the back of the room, shot twice in the head by some unknown adventurer at some point over the last year.

When they didn't find anything overtly threatening among the shadows, they left the galley and moved to the unlocked door. David opened it and peered in. His flashlight revealed a dusty stairwell bathed in darkness. It revealed another thing. As he stepped in, he caught a whiff of the unmistakable scent of the undead. Not exactly a revelation, but he hated it all the same. Part of him had been hoping it was just a squirrel or raccoon or something that had gotten in upstairs and made some noise, but he couldn't ignore that smell.

SMG at the fore, finger on the trigger, he tried to make himself relax as he ascended. As unlikely as it was becoming, David had to remember that there could be people in here, survivors like himself. Trapped, possibly, by the undead. It seemed improbable, but not impossible. The stairwell went up to a landing, then doubled back on itself, leading to the second story. David hit the landing and made the turn, aiming up.

The door up there was open, almost as if beckoning.

He swallowed and forced himself onward and upward. As he came to stand at the latest threshold, the comforting sounds of the others behind him,

David found himself staring down another long corridor. This one ran the length of the structure, bisecting the second story. There were about a dozen doors along the walls. Distantly, opposite his current position, he saw a window through which muted gray sunlight came.

He became aware of a new sound, then.

At first, he couldn't place it. Tapping, a lot of quiet tapping. Then it came to him: rain. It had started to rain outside. Under normal circumstances he'd be pretty happy about that particular development but here it only served to make the atmosphere even more ominous. Especially when thunder rumbled and lightning flared across the far window. David took a cautious step into the hallway, looking towards the nearest open door.

Gradually, he made his way over to it. Nervously, he peered in through the open doorway, as the door itself was nowhere to be seen. He peered around the corner with the SMG lighting and leading the way. What might once have been a shared office was a revealed.

He spied a desk off in the far right corner and another to his immediate left, as well as a door near it, also open. David finished scoping out the room from where he stood and then slipped in. Ellie came in behind him as he moved over to the other door.

"Let's clear this place," he said just loud enough to be heard, "room by–"

David froze as he got a view of the next room. A wildcat stood in it, almost like it was waiting for him. It opened its mouth and issued a shriek. David immediately sighted it and fired off a burst of bullets that went into its big, blood-smeared mouth and blew out the back of its misshapen skull in a spray of blood and brains.

Immediately, a dozen more shrieks went up.

"Fuck!" Ellie snapped.

"Val! Ellie! Cover the hallway! Jennifer watch the stairwell!" he screamed as he stepped into the next room and cleared it with a quick sweep of his SMG.

They all snapped off replies as they got into position. He could hear the sound of scrabbling claws, the wildcats coming for them, the dinner bell sounded.

They were no doubt eager for fresh meat.

The scrabbling claws drew closer, and there were a lot of them. David readjusted his grip on the SMG, standing a little ways into the second room, what seemed to be another office, and aiming directly for the doorway across the room. He didn't have to wait long.

Within a few seconds, Ellie and Val opened fire, Ellie's pistol banging away and Val's shotgun booming like a cannon. He saw movement and one of the wildcats slipped into the room with him. He didn't give it a chance, cutting down the awful, malformed thing in a spray of gunfire. Another appeared to take its place, all patchy fur and stringy muscle.

A line of bloody holes opened up across its chest and went up, splitting its head and spraying the walls around it with blood. Even as it fell, another one slipped into the room, and there was another behind it. Cursing, David kept up the fire.

He emptied his submachine gun pumping red hot lead into their awful undead bodies, spilling more blood as he killed them. As his gun clicked dry and the fourth awful creature fell dead, he hastily reloaded, ejecting the spent magazine and slapping in a fresh one. Bringing it back up, he realized the other gunfire had fallen silent. They waited. A few seconds passed. Something shrieked, a gunshot sounded, then silence fell again.

Finally, after another ten seconds of nothing, David let himself relax slightly. "Clear?" he called to the others.

"Clear," Val reported.

"Clear here," Jennifer said.

"Looks clear," Ellie replied.

"Good. Let's get to searching."

They broke back up into their original groups and each took one side of the hallway. David and Ellie poked through the pair of offices they'd come through initially, making sure they hadn't missed anything obvious, then moved on. The rest of their side was taken up by a single large area that was mostly empty. It looked like it might once have been a storage area, but it had obviously been being used as a feeding ground or sleeping area, or both, by the pack of wildcats that called this place home.

The windows had all been broken out and he could easily envision them coming and going this way. Once they cleared it, they checked in with Val and Jennifer, who reported seeing another bathroom, a pair offices, and a room packed with old equipment that Jennifer said was mostly replacement parts for the machinery.

Which was obviously a good sign, though a lot of it was rusted, broken, or missing.

"Let's finish our search, then we can look for the key to the basement while you check out the equipment," David suggested.

"Fine by me," Jennifer replied.

They moved back down the hallway to the initial

door they'd come through and ascended to the third and final story. Here they found what seemed to be the control room for the water filtration plant. There were a lot of broken monitors around, several chairs scattered across a handful of interconnected rooms, as well as lots of desks and other furniture.

They found no other wildcats or any other undead lurking around. After they'd made sure that the place was secure, or as secure as it was going to get, Jennifer and Val headed back downstairs to the spare equipment room. Jennifer began sorting through it all while David and Ellie stayed in the third floor and started looking for the key to the basement and any other useful items.

"So, David..." Ellie said about five minutes into their search.

"Yeah?" he replied.

"I've been meaning to ask you something. It occurred to me a few days ago. I don't know why it took me so long to think about it, but...I guess it's a weird question."

"Shoot."

She laughed. "Yeah, I guess we're past weird questions at this point. Okay, so, here's the thing: healthy sperm is rare nowadays. At least from what I've been able to figure out. I mean like half of guys are shooting blanks, I think. Something like that. And at least some of those have not healthy sperm thanks to the virus. So you're kind of a rarity. I mean, provided the kid comes out healthy and not deformed or anything." She paused and glanced at him, wincing. "Sorry."

He sighed. "It's fine."

She cleared her throat and went back to searching. "Um, so, my question was: how would you feel about it if a woman who wanted to get pregnant came to you and asked you to knock her up?" she asked.

David stopped searching for a moment, considering her words. He had to admit, he felt an immediate thrill of lust, intense lust, at the scenario.

"Well...under the right circumstances, I'd be amenable to it," he replied finally.

Ellie smirked. "The right circumstances being?"

"That all parties involved are informed and okay with it, to begin with."

"It's two people."

He shook his head. "What? No. *Obviously* Cait needs to be aware of this. As well as Evie and April. You."

She hesitated. "Me? Really?"

"Duh. I fucking love you, genius. This would be an important decision. You need to be at the very least aware that it's happening and have a voice in the matter."

"I...see," she murmured.

"What, did you think I just kept you around for the pussy?" he asked.

She heaved a sigh and rolled her eyes. "Piss off," she replied. "And *no*. Obviously I know we're, you know, *really* good friends who love each other and have sex. I just...I'm still getting used to this. I know it's been months, but I'm just...still getting used to the idea that I'm part of not just a community, but this inner circle of love and friendship and polyamory we have going. It's...new. So continue," she said, brushing him with her tail in passing.

"So yeah, all parties, people important to me and people important to them, would at least need to be involved and, while *ultimately* I guess I can't speak for people they know, because the bottom line is it would be their decision to get pregnant, I have to admit I *would* be more reluctant if, like, they were with someone and that someone didn't want it to happen. And I'd probably need to like the person and feel like they were going to be a good parent. I mean, I know that's a roll of the dice, but I'm not going to agree to give someone a kid who's obviously going to be a shitty parent."

"Fair enough. So if all the stars aligned and everything's on the up and up, you'd shoot your load into another woman and get her pregnant?" Ellie asked.

"Yeah."

"What if she didn't want you involved in the kid's life at all?"

"I mean...that'd be fair. Honestly, I have my hands full enough as it is, so I think that'd actually be preferable. I mean, my involvement afterward would need to be ironed out beforehand, but yeah, I'd be down for that," he replied.

"Huh." She paused and looked at him. "You really like the idea of getting women pregnant, don't you?"

"Yes. You know this about me," he replied.

She laughed. "Yeah, I guess so. Cait told me about the first time you fucked. Do you know why that is? Why you're into that? I mean, I know why you're into pregnant women. Their tits and their asses and hips and thighs all get bigger and they just generally get hotter. Like, fuck, I didn't think Cait could get hotter but holy *shit* is she like three times as hot as she was."

He laughed. "Fuck yes, she is. But as for why? I don't know. Probably because humans evolved to want to reproduce, and this is how the brain translates it. I just *really* like the idea of shooting my seed into a woman's womb and knocking her up. Plus, I have to admit, I'd *really* enjoy the opportunity to do it again, because this time around, I'd actually know that A) it was going to happen and B) we were intentionally trying to do it. I imagine that would be insanely fucking hot."

"Oh hell yes it would," Ellie replied. "If you somehow find yourself in this position, *please* try hard to get her to let me watch."

"I imagine most women in my life are going to ask the same thing. We'll need a goddamned auditorium," he muttered.

Ellie laughed. "Yeah, that's true. Does it freak you out? Fucking for an audience?"

"Not anymore. I mean, not if it's all people I know. It'd be different if it was a bunch of strangers, or even non-strangers, like people from Haven. I like it if you're all watching. You and Ashley and Lara and other women I've fucked."

"I like it, too. Watching and being watched. I imagine you and I make for spectacular viewing material while we fuck," Ellie replied.

"That's what I've been told."

They got back to focusing on their job and continued their search of the third story. They only managed to find a handful of useful items, mostly some spare parts that Ellie recognized, a few tools, and a little stash of bullets, a knife, and some medical supplies that someone had long ago tucked away in a long-forgotten desk drawer. After that, they returned to Jennifer to check up on her, found that she wasn't close to finished, and resumed their search, this time of the second story, always on the lookout for any and all keys.

An hour passed in the rainy gloom.

Two hours passed. Then three.

David and Ellie and, after Jennifer promised she'd be fine on her own, Val, scoured the second floor, and then the first. They were thorough, and managed to turn up not just an appreciable supply of useful materials, some survival gear and food, and parts and tools that would be useful in their project, but a half-dozen keys. By the time they were finished, so was Jennifer. They all gathered in the equipment room.

"So, what's the story?" David asked, glancing out the nearest window. It was still raining outside, thought not as bad as before. Now it was just a sullen drizzle that saturated the landscape beyond the dirty glass.

"The good news is that I managed to find about half of what I need. Unfortunately, the rest of the stuff here is broken or incompatible with what we've got. But this is good. Did you find the key to the basement?" she asked.

"I hope so," he replied, patting his pocket where the collection of keys jingled.

"Well, let's see what we can see," Val said.

They moved back through the structure until they had gathered at the locked basement door. David reached into his pocket and fished out the keys. Right away, it was clear that three of them wouldn't work, as they were too large. Probably to vehicles that the long dead staff had abandoned. He pocketed them anyway, as he never knew when they might be useful, and then tried the others. The second one slid in and turned.

The padlock unlocked and he took it off, then

slowly pulled open the door. Val stood at the entrance, aiming her shotgun and flashlight down as the door opened. Ellie and Jennifer remained behind them, covering the rear. As David finished opening the door, making sure to stand well clear of it in case anything came shrieking up, nothing happened.

"Clear," Val said.

He peered in. A dank concrete stairway descended into the earth.

"I'll take point," Val said when no one spoke up. Still no one spoke up, happy enough to let her take that wretched responsibility. As it was, David wasn't too keen on the idea of heading down into this dark, miserable environment.

They moved in a single file down the stairwell. The place stank, though it was an old, fetid smell. Like oily sewage that had been locked up for years. They reached the bottom of the stairwell and Val opened up the door they found there.

"Looks like a big place," she muttered as she peered through.

"It should be," Jennifer replied.

"No sign of hostiles, but there's a *lot* of places to hide down here."

"We'll take it nice and slow," David replied.

Val stepped inside, making room. David came in behind her. Jennifer was next, and Ellie brought up the rear. David shined his light as he looked around. It *was* a big place. The stairway let out onto a metal platform that overlooked the basement. To their right was a cargo lift, just a simple, flat elevator probably meant to shift heavy machinery and equipment to the ground level, and to the left was a stairwell leading down to the main floor. It looked kind of like a factory down there, with a lot of big, hulking pieces of equipment and several large tubes and tanks.

"So this is what we're looking for?" David asked quietly.

"Yep," Jennifer replied.

"How long do you think this'll take?"

"I honestly don't know," Jennifer admitted.

"All right. We'll sweep the area first. We should stick together," Ellie said.

"Yeah," David agreed. He resisted the urge to groan in frustration. "Okay, let's get this out of the way so we can go home."

They made their way slowly down the stairwell, which creaked and groaned beneath their weight, and came down onto the stone floor. David hadn't seen any movement among the shadows from his overhead view, but that didn't mean they were alone. They came down into the area beyond the stairway and spread out, playing their lights across the dark area. There were no windows down here in the underground, and the lights were long dead.

"What's the best way to do this?" Jennifer murmured.

"Make a sweep of the outer perimeter," Val replied, "then do the same for the inner section of the room."

"Sounds good, you wanna lead?" he asked.

"Yep," she replied, and set off. "Keep close, but not too close."

They set off into the darkness, their movements slow and cautious. David began to sweat before long, not just from the close environment as they passed between large pieces of machinery, but mainly from the tension that began rising from the dark, claustrophobic atmosphere of the treatment plant basement.

He kept listening for some sound, for a noise to give away anything that might be hiding down here. Normally they weren't dead silent, except for the stalkers. *Was* there anything down here? It was possible they were alone.

But he just couldn't help but feel like there was something down here.

None of them spoke as they pressed on, moving along first the wall nearest the stairway they'd descended, and then, when they hit a corner, moving along the left wall. They walked slowly and carefully between the equipment and work areas and machinery, Val stopping to check around every corner, shining her light into every shadowy niche. Every time she did that, David tensed up, expecting the worst.

But nothing happened.

They hit the next corner and began moving along the next wall. It went like this for a grueling twenty minutes, shifting along the exterior and finding nothing, eventually circling back around to their starting point. From there, they moved into the central area. They moved among a cluster of machinery and work areas, keeping tense and ready for action. But at the end of another fifteen minute investigation, they determined that they were alone.

"Fuck," Ellie whispered, leaning heavily against a nearby metal cylinder. "I thought for sure there'd be something down here."

"Same," David said, trying to relax.

"Sometimes it's just an anticlimax," Val replied. "Honestly, I look forward to these."

"Yeah," David murmured, nodding. "Okay, Jennifer, grab what you need, I want to get the fuck out of here as soon as possible."

"On it," she replied, and headed for the nearest piece of machinery.

CHAPTER NINE

Despite the long walk up the river, the harrowing fight with the wildcats at the plant, the lengthy search of the building, and the long walk back home, David felt good. Honestly, he felt great. They were making progress, and nothing seemed to feel quite as good as making progress. Okay, that wasn't really true.

Sex felt better than making progress.

But there was a deep satisfaction to setting goals and completing them.

Jennifer had filled out her list of tools and spare parts and crucial components, and then some. She'd loaded down their backpacks with as much gear as she had been able to find, stuff that would not only fix the water purification machine and keep it running for, ideally, years, but other parts and tools that would help fix up the plumbing system of the new settlement and likely help in other, yet unforeseen ways.

They walked along the river until they had arrived at the new settlement, where they found a bustle of activity. Close to a dozen and a half people were moving around within the fenced-off part of the settlement. Some stood guard, a few others were in the process of cleaning out the buildings, bringing out trash or old furniture that was too broken to be repaired and could be reduced to spare parts or kindling, and the rest were fixing up the houses.

There had been enough construction material leftover at Haven that they could begin reparation of the houses they had managed to secure so far, and David felt his good mood boosted even higher at the sight.

Everyone looked happy, and busy.

He hoped that they were feeling what he had felt during the reconstruction project that had turned the old campgrounds into Haven, that unique elation and joy that came from putting work into a place that was going to be your home. He had learned that there was a special kind of happiness that came from personally putting work into the place you were going to live in or even around. And he was glad to see that most of the people here were from Lori's and Val's group.

He imagined that not too many would feel like moving from Haven. There were more adventurous types like Ashley and Ellie who might be into it, and those who had been chafing under the overcrowding problem, but for the most part people were happy with Haven.

They were greeted by happy people as they came up to the gate, where Ashley and one of the people from Val's group were standing guard, chatting about something. As soon as she saw her, Ashley shot to her feet, ran to Ellie, and gave her a long hug and a kiss.

"Tell me you're done and you're going to stay here with me," she said. "Because I've missed you too much today."

Ellie laughed and hugged her back. "I'm done and I'm going to stay here with you."

"Thank you," Ashley whispered, and hugged her again. Then she stepped back and growled in frustration. "Dammit, being in love can be *so* annoying! I get so miserable when you aren't around for more than a few hours, it's awful."

"I know the feeling," Ellie replied.

"Yeah," David murmured, already thinking of Cait, and Evie and April back at Haven.

"Did it go well?" They glanced over at the new

voice and saw Lara approaching. For a moment, David couldn't respond because he was too distracted by how she looked.

Lara was stunning.

At some point, she had largely abandoned wearing her military fatigues. Now, she had donned a kerchief tied over her head, a simple green t-shirt, and some jeans that were ripped off at the knee. She had clearly been working hard, as she'd sweated through most of the clothes, and her shirt clung very pleasantly to her wonderfully fit frame. Though he did notice that she filled out her clothes just a little bit more than when they'd first met.

She especially filled out her pants more.

"Good," he said finally.

"Yeah?"

"We found the parts, and some spares, and all the tools we need," Jennifer replied. "I'm going to get to work on it now."

"Excellent! I don't suppose there's any chance of a shower anytime soon..."

"Unfortunately not. It's going to be, at minimum, days. More, if I have to go other places. Speaking of which..." She looked at David. "I had a thought."

"Yeah?"

"We live in a forest. I know how to convert trees into usable lumber, it's just a matter of people and the proper tools. I was thinking we could go to the logging camp in the forest near Lima Company's fort but, if I remember right, that was destroyed while we were dealing with the stalker infestation..." Jennifer said.

"I know where there's a second logging camp," Lara said. They all looked at her. "We found it while scouting to the south, around the other side of the mountain. It's not far from that site we had to bomb to seal off the tunnels during that operation. We tried to investigate further a few times, but it was always too overrun with stalkers. Now that their numbers are way down, maybe we can send a team out and investigate."

"All right, I'm down for that. Would we need the truck for that?" he asked.

"No, with a few strong people, we should be able to haul it back," Lara replied. "It's not like we'd have a massive operation here, but we'd be able to chop down trees and turn them into lumber without *too* much trouble with some of this stuff."

"I'll write up a list of things you'll need," Jennifer said.

"Well, I obviously need to go," Lara said, "given I know the way there."

"I'm down," Val said. "I'm going to go spend the night back at the hunting lodge, but I'll be here in the morning."

"I'll go," David said.

"I would, but with Lara leaving, I think we'll need another gun here to help defend," Ellie said. "Plus, I imagine Ashley would turn violent if I left again tomorrow."

"I might," she growled.

"You know, I bet Evie would like a chance to go, and she's plenty strong," David said.

"Very true. What about Akila? If we're going into potential stalker territory, I'd like to have her along," Lara asked.

"She's still out hunting," Ashley replied, "but she said she'd be back tonight. When she returns, I'll update her on the situation. I'm sure she'd be glad to go."

"Perfect. So we've got our team. Let's unload and get back home. I'm sure Cait's going crazy by now," David said.

"She's not the only one," Lara murmured, glancing at him significantly.

He felt a blast of lust hit him like a punch to the gut and struggled to keep his focus. "Let's hurry," he added.

...

Fifteen minutes later, David and Lara were walking back to Haven.

"Lara...are you happier here, with us?" he asked, glancing at her. He hadn't quite meant to ask the question that bluntly, but sometimes that's how it happened.

"Of course," she replied immediately. Then she laughed. "Isn't it obvious?"

"I mean, I guess. I don't know, I just worry that you miss the military lifestyle."

She lost a little bit of her smile. "I do," she admitted. "To a certain degree. But you and the others didn't take it from me. It wasn't necessarily a sacrifice that I made. What I had with Lima Company was no longer quite the military lifestyle, or at least not the one that I had learned to love. Stern had turned it into something else. I could see clear nepotism at work in the ranks. In the military, in *my* military, it's fair.

"Now, to be sure, those who screw up due to their own shortsighted stupidity get punished, and get crap assignments, but it was rare we had that happen in Lima Company. No, the crap assignments, the shit that people didn't want to do or hated doing, were meant to be distributed evenly and fairly. So we all shared the necessary misery among ourselves. For a while, it was like that. Stern was fair. Tough, but fair.

"But that changed near the end. I could see him honing in on people he didn't like, forcing them to do the miserable assignments while giving the ones who'd gained his favor easy jobs, or no jobs sometimes. I couldn't stomach that. As his second in command, I did my best to even it out, but he grew to hate me.

"Partially because of my sympathy for your group, partially because it always seemed like I was trying to be a salve to his brutish authority, something he tried to cloak as a 'necessary evil', when we all knew what he was playing at." She sighed heavily. "I miss what it was like before, but by the time I left, it was gone regardless. But even if it wasn't...I wish that I would have made the choice to come here anyway."

"Really?"

"Yes. I'm the happiest I've ever been, because there isn't really a compromise that needs to be made. Everywhere I've lived, every group I've run with, there's always been some sort of compromise. Usually it was 'suck up to the boss to make them happy or suffer the consequences', but sometimes it was other things. For a while, it wasn't that way with Lima Company, but not only do I not have to make compromises at Haven: I'm happy here. I was more...satisfied, with Lima Company. But now I'm happy. I'm both. And, to be honest..." she hesitated and glanced at him. She looked uncomfortable and vulnerable.

He waited, giving her time.

She swallowed. "To be honest, David, I've always had poor luck with romance. I mean, I've had boyfriends in the past who made me happy. They were usually great in some way...but they were also usually really shitty in another way. Like that compromise I was going on about. He'd be great in bed, but an asshole when the mood took him, and it took him often. Or a guy would be nice, but terrible at survival and overly reliant on me.

"Kind and supportive to me, but then I'd find out he's a raging fucking racist against any inhumans. But with you, and with Cait, I don't...have to compromise. I love you, and I love Cait, and I never thought that I could–" she laughed and blinked a few times, reaching up, brushing away tears, "I never thought I'd love two people at once, not romantically, nor that one of them would be a woman, but...here we are."

"I love you too, Lara," he said, reaching out. She immediately took his hand. "And I know Cait loves you. We all do."

"I know. I just...I'm nervous, honestly."

"Why?"

"We have these interconnecting relationships. You and Evie and April and Cait are together. But also Ellie and Ashley are together, but Ellie is *really* close with you and Cait. And then I'm with you and Cait but no one else. I just...worry it's all too good to be true. That it's going to fall apart somehow, someway," she murmured.

"I understand how you feel, actually," David replied. "I was really nervous about that in the beginning myself. In some ways, I still am. But I don't think it's going to happen. I mean, we'll fight. All of us will at one point or another. That's just life. But we're probably going to be okay. And if one of us or more than one of us leaves or breaks up, I think it'll be a decision that was reached maturely and responsibly, and not something done out of enraged passion or a moment of anger. We'll do it because it will be, unfortunately, the most mature choice to make. And honestly I just hope I don't have to lose any of you. You're all wonderful."

"Thanks," she murmured. She laughed and squeezed his hand again. "It's still so weird when I tell you or Cait that I love you, or you say it to me, like...it's illicit. Like I have to worry about the wrong person overhearing it. Like we'll get in trouble."

"I understand," he said. He could see Haven up ahead, and as they caught sight of it, he felt a pulse of intense desire pass between them. David looked at her. "So, do you wanna–"

"Yes," she replied immediately. "I want to go grab Cait, go upstairs, lock ourselves in, and just fuck. I'm *so* goddamned horny. I've been horny all day but I've been too busy working on the new place to even masturbate and just...I *need* your cock inside me."

"Well all right, then let's go," he replied, and they picked up the pace.

They checked in with the gate guard and, after making sure nothing of any significance had happened while they were out, hurried through the settlement and got into the main office. They hurried up the stairs and came into the dining area, where they found Evie and April sitting at the main table, looking over several papers.

"Hey! How'd it go?" Evie asked.

"Great! We found all the parts and tools we need, Jennifer and Ellie are at the new settlement for the night, and Val went home to the hunting grounds for now," David replied, trying not to rush through the report. He had a raging erection right now and wanted desperately to hop into bed with Lara and Cait. "Um, before I forget, we're going to another logging camp on the other side of the mountain tomorrow to see if we can find some tools to help us chop down trees to make lumber. Do you want to go?" he asked.

"Honestly, yeah, I'd like to go. I've mostly got this stuff wrapped up and I could use a break away from Haven for a bit," Evie replied.

"Where's Cait?" Lara asked.

Evie smirked. "Upstairs 'reading'," she said, rolling her eyes. "Really she's just masturbating and waiting for you since April and I were too busy to help her out. I can tell you two are extremely antsy to get naked and sweaty, so why don't you join her and April and I will get to work on dinner. You can come down and help once you've had your orgasms."

"Thank you! Love you! Both of you!" David replied, then he grabbed Lara's hand and dashed off to the stairs. Both women laughed after them as they hurried upstairs.

As they approached the door leading to his, Evie's, and Cait's bedroom, they could hear her moaning in pleasure. He knocked rapidly on the door.

"Shit," he heard her mutter. "Who is it?"

"Me and Lara!" he replied.

"Fuck, finally! Get in here!"

He all but threw open the door and stepped inside. Cait was laid out on the bed, above the blankets, completely naked and sweaty, face flushed, legs open. It was obvious that she'd already given herself at least one orgasm, probably more.

"Fucking took you long enough," she said as Lara shut the door and then they both hurried over to the washbasin.

"Sorry, honey, it was a long day," David replied.

"Hurry up!" she said, sounding truly exasperated. "It's bad right now."

"Okay, okay," he replied, stripping out of his clothes and washing up as quickly as he could. His eyes kept straying to her. She looked like a sex demon or a goddess of fertile lust laying there like that, her belly swollen, her thighs smooth and pale and so wonderfully thick, hips fantastically broad, tits amazingly huge.

God, but were her tits just fucking massive.

"Wow, Lara," Cait said as they washed up. "You are looking just *so* good right now."

"Really?" she replied, glancing down at herself.

David looked over at her. She did look extremely good right now, her fit yet now more pleasantly padded body smooth and tanned in most places.

"God yes," he agreed.

"I'm positive I've put on weight since coming here," she murmured as she kept washing.

"You have," Cait agreed.

"Wow, thanks."

Cait's flush deepened. "Oh, fuck, sorry. That wasn't a shot, Lara. I meant it like in a good way. At this point I've come to believe that putting on some weight isn't always a bad thing. And not just because I'm pregnant. I mean David put on weight since I first met him."

"Yeah, but that's all muscle, right?" Lara replied. "And it's not like I was super skinny before."

"Probably not *all* of it," he said. "And I agree with her. You look just...divine."

She laughed. "I see. Well, I guess when it comes to how you look, what matters most is how hot the people you're fucking think you are," she said with a shrug.

Cait seemed to have calmed somewhat as she sat up. "It's important that you feel good about how you look, but it's also important that you recognize when you're obsessing over body image. I mean, you can still run all over the place, haul stuff around all day, fight and kick ass when it's necessary, right? You're not slowing down, I imagine."

"No, I'm not," Lara agreed. "Well, maybe a *little,* but I think that's more due to age than anything else. I'm just about thirty seven now and while that's not old by any stretch of the imagination, your thirties are supposed to be where age begins to rear its ugly head. And I'm certainly not adhering to as rigid a schedule and workout regimen as I once did. You fucking hedonists have gotten to me with your good food and sex and long, sleepy mornings."

"Is it truly so bad a lifestyle?" Cait asked, grinning.

She heaved a sigh. "No, it isn't. It's great. It just comes at a cost."

"Doesn't everything?" David asked.

"Yeah, I guess so. And honestly it's worth it to be here with you all," Lara replied.

"Good. Now, enough philosophy and life lessons, get the fuck over here," Cait said, her sexual impatience returning.

They finished up and got into bed with her. As soon as he was within grasping range, Cait grasped him and pulled him close to her. They began kissing with an intense passion as they came in contact, and her touch was electrifying. He began groping her massive, pregnant breasts as their lips locked and tongues started to twist and dance together.

She moaned as they made out. Lara settled on her

other side and ran her own hands across Cait's wonderfully voluptuous body. After making out with David for a bit, Cait immediately switched to Lara, feeling up her big, firm breasts and making out with her with an immediately intense passion.

David slipped lower and began to suck on one of her big breasts while at the same time sliding a hand down her smooth, thick thigh and in between her legs, seeking her clit and, upon finding it, beginning to rub it.

"Oh!" Cait cried as the pleasure hit her like an electric shock. She let out a long, lusty moan of satisfaction as he began to pleasure her, massaging her clit with the tip of his finger. "This is *exactly* what I've been fucking looking forward to all day..."

"It's only going to get better," Lara replied, smiling and lowering herself along with David. She began sucking on Cait's other breast and reached down, her hand joining his. She slipped a finger into Cait's vagina and the redhead shuddered violently and began panting heavily.

"Oh fuck it feels so good," she whispered, her voice trembling along with her body.

That was another change that David was glad to see: Lara was more sexually confident. It hadn't taken her all that long to get confident with him, but that was because she was more familiar with men and it became pretty clear quite quickly that he was utterly in lust with her. So her natural confidence in other aspects of life transferred pretty quickly into their sexual sessions. But he knew Cait intimidated her intensely.

Not just because she was extraordinarily beautiful and extremely confident herself, but also because Lara had always danced around the notion that she was bisexual. Cait was...an interesting person to explore that possibility with, he imagined. But it seemed to have worked out for the best, because Lara threw herself into their threesomes and sex with each of them individually without hesitation or uncertainty now.

They pleasured Cait for several minutes. Licking and sucking on her huge, pale breasts while satisfying her pregnant pussy, Lara fucking her with two fingers, David massaging her clit with an increasing pressure and speed.

They made her come three times.

After the third time, she gently stopped them and caught her breath. "Okay," she whispered, panting, "okay, Lara...let's take care of our man."

"All right," Lara replied, grinning over her pale body at David.

"Then I'll take care of you," Cait added, smiling and running a hand down her side.

"Well, so far, no one has eaten pussy as good as you," Lara said. "So yes please."

Cait laughed and kissed her, then looked at David. "Up," she said.

He stood up. Given her pregnant state, they'd found that it was easiest for her to suck dick by getting on her knees. Lara joined her as she knelt before him. Looking down at them both, these two naked, amazingly beautiful women as they stared up at him, preparing to pleasure him, gave him an intense thrill of lust and an almost dizzying sense of dreamlike reality. Even now, after all this time, it still didn't seem real.

Lara cupped his balls in her soft, warm grasp and began to massage them slowly as Cait encircled his shaft with her thumb and first two fingers. Both women leaned in and began to slowly licked the head, causing him to groan loudly as the pleasure hit him like a bullet. Not just the pleasure of their hot, wet tongues dragging across the most sensitive part of his body, but the sight of their beautiful, upturned faces as they licked his cock. They had both gotten very good at pleasuring him, learning his body as he had learned theirs over the past several months.

Cait opened her mouth and took his dick into it, closing her luscious red lips around his shaft and beginning to bob her head. He groaned louder, laying a hand against her soft red hair. She'd let it grow out over the past few months and he thought she looked sexier than ever as a result.

Cait slipped her lips up over his head again and again for a solid minute, her eyes closed as she sucked his dick and filled him with a rapturous bliss, then she passed it over to Lara. The sexy brunette took over oral duties, bobbing her own head as she continued massaging his balls in her hot grasp, increasing the pleasure and filling him with a hot bliss.

They kept going like that back and forth, taking turns sucking him off, until the desire to be inside of their perfect pussies was too great.

"Okay, sex now," he said, panting.

"You got it. Lara, on your back," Cait said.

"Yes, ma'am," Lara murmured as she laid down and spread her legs. Cait got onto her hands and knees between Lara's thick thighs and David immediately sank to his own knees behind Cait. As his redheaded lover lowered her head into Lara's crotch and began to pleasure her with her skilled tongue, eliciting moans of pure ecstasy from her, David ran his hands over Cait's fat, pale ass. He marveled over how remarkably sexy she looked and then quickly began pushing his cock into her slippy, steaming hot pussy.

Both of them moaned in mutual gratification as they began to fuck like animals.

Sliding into her was a study in pure bliss, of absolute sexual gratification. Even after fucking her dozens, probably hundreds of times at this point, he still was completely, totally, wholly in fucking love with the feeling of penetrating her bare pussy. Even more so now that she was this far along into the pregnancy. It seemed to make her even hotter inside, and certainly tighter.

He settled his hands on her big, pale hips as he began driving into her just how she liked it, quickly amping up to a hard and fast pace, and listened to her let out muffled grunts and groans of pleasure as she ate Lara out. Lara's face twisted in pure ecstasy as Cait put her tongue to use. She looked phenomenally sexy, nude with her legs spread wide, her hands running slowly through Cait's vibrantly red hair. She was panting, her breasts swaying and shifting.

It made for fantastic viewing as he pounded Cait from the back.

Before long, Lara's whole body clenched and she began moaning more quickly, signaling that Cait was on her way to giving their lover an orgasm, and as David watched, she suddenly went over the edge and was consumed by a full-body climax. She let out a strangled sound of absolute pleasure and went rigid, her hips jerking as she came. Cait kept fingering her, furiously fucking her orgasming pussy with two of her fingers as Lara squirted and cried out.

"Come on!" Cait growled. "Fucking come for me!"

"Oh! Fuck! *Cait! OH MY GOD!*" she cried as she was overwhelmed by mindless ecstasy.

David watched, enraptured, as he kept fucking Cait, the sound of his hips slapping against her big ass mixing in with Lara's cries of bliss.

Her orgasm went on for a good while, and when she was done, she went slack, panting, almost gasping for breath, staring at the ceiling.

"Lara," David said after a bit.

"Uh-huh?" she murmured.

"Get up. Next to Cait. Hands and knees," he replied.

She looked down at him, a smile coming onto her face. "Yes, sir."

She got up from underneath Cait and settled into place next to Cait on her hands and knees. As soon as she was in position, David pulled out of Cait and shifted over to Lara. He slid into her fantastically slick, wet vagina and began stroking into her. She let out a low, satisfied moan as they started to fuck.

"Oh wow that is *so* fucking good..." she groaned.

"Damn right it is," David replied, giving her thick, fit ass a hard smack. She groaned again and pushed back against him.

David lost himself in the two women as he made love to them. He pounded Lara from the back, shoving his whole rock-hard cock into her again and again, burying himself in that sweet, fit military vagina as he grasped her broad, firm hips, and then pulling out and switching over to Cait and just fucking her brains out.

There was an intensely deep pleasure and satisfaction to fucking two women at the same time, being able to switch between the two of them whenever he wanted, having both of them willing to get fucked by him and just taking his cock raw.

He fucked Lara until he got another orgasm out of her, pounding her while reaching up under her and rubbing her clit vigorously. He listened to her cry out and moan, felt her shudder and spasm from the intense pleasure he was giving her, and then groaned as he felt a hot stream of her sex juices begin to come out of her as her vaginal muscles convulsed and fluttered around him.

David kept screwing her hard and fast as she came, just pounding the fuck out of her orgasming pussy all the way through it. When she was done, he pulled out of her and patted her ass a few times, signaling that he was okay with her being done.

She fell forward and rolled onto her side, looking sleepy and deeply satisfied.

"Can we do anal?" he asked as he moved over to Cait.

"Yes," Cait replied immediately, her hand going under the pillows and coming back out with a bottle of lubrication. She passed it back to him and he quickly lubed his cock up. Once that was done, he tossed the bottle aside and began working himself slowly into Cait's huge, pale ass. Since she'd become noticeably pregnant, anal sex with her was better than ever. Maybe it was just because he loved how her ass looked with how big it had gotten, but it really felt better. She groaned and pushed against him as he worked his way into her.

Her ass was so fucking tight and he knew that like most other times he fucked her in the ass, he wasn't going to last long.

It was just too good.

Lara watched as they started screwing once he'd gotten completely into her ass. He began stroking into it over and over again, the pleasure eating into him.

"Oh fuck, you feel *huge...*" Cait groaned, hanging her head as she took his dick.

"Your ass is so fucking tight, babe..." he moaned in response, reaching up under her and grabbing her big tits. He squeezed and groped them as he fucked her in the ass. Within another half minute, he was coming. He cried out as he started blasting his load into her, spurting his seed up her thick, broad ass and moaning as the pleasure washed over and through him, consuming him whole.

He felt blinded and deafened, the raw ecstasy of the orgasm overwhelming all of his senses. He laid against Cait, though even in his state he was careful not to lean too heavily on her. He came a huge amount into her, feeling his whole body writhing and contracting with the ebb and flow of the orgasm. It felt like it went on for a while.

Finally, as he finished up, he carefully pulled out of her and fell onto his back.

"Satisfied?" he asked the two women.

"Yeah," Lara said.

"For now," Cait replied.

"God, I hope you stay this horny after the pregnancy," he murmured.

She laughed. "Who knows. Maybe."

They laid there together for a bit, nude and sweaty and getting their breaths back, basking in the post orgasmic glow and enjoying each other's company.

Eventually, they began to get cleaned up to go help with dinner.

CHAPTER TEN

David, Evie, and Lara turned up at the new settlement bright and early the next day.

After last night, (and this morning), he was feeling pretty refreshed and ready to go. This time around, at least, he was happy that they wouldn't have to trek all the way out of the region to get to where they were going. The walk there was little more than perhaps an hour-long hike around the mountain. They found Val chatting with Akila just inside the gate as they approached and the two women stood up and stretched.

"We ready?" David asked.

"We're ready," Val replied, and Akila nodded.

"What about the list from Jennifer?" Lara asked.

Val reached into a pocket and pulled out a folded-up piece of paper. She passed it to them and they looked it over. David was impressed. Not only had she given them a list, she'd made small but detailed drawings of what each tool would look like.

"Nice," he said, folding it back up and passing it to Val.

"You should hold onto it, it'll get lost or ripped up if I hang onto it," she said. He shrugged and put it into his pocket. "I can haul stuff for days but when it comes to papers, fuck, I don't know what it is. They always get fucked up."

"That sucks. It must be hard to navigate in unfamiliar areas if you can't keep your hands on a map," Lara replied as they began to walk away from the settlement.

"Yep. I had to get really good at navigation," Val replied.

"Did anything happen overnight?" David asked.

"At the settlement? No, not really. Two stalker attacks that we put down with ease. Otherwise no. Someone was fucking, though. One of our people shacked up with one of your people, so...good to see we're compatible."

"Oh...well that *is* nice," Evie murmured.

Val smirked suddenly as they headed into the forest, making for the mountain. "Lori was asking after you," she said, poking David's shoulder.

"Oh yeah?" he replied.

"Yep. She wants to fuck you, I can tell."

"Did you tell her we fucked?" he asked.

"Not in so many words. I hinted, teased her a little. Don't worry, she won't be angry. And it's not like she has some policy of not fucking guys I've already fucked. But I guess I just feel a little bad. I fuck with such impunity sometimes, or at least it seems like that to her, and she's so...I want to say picky, but she isn't. She just has standards, and that's fair, but it also makes it harder to find people who meet those standards nowadays."

"Which I'm sure David absolutely does meet them," Evie murmured.

"Yes! He does. Which is why I wholeheartedly support the two of you fucking like rabbits. I've been giving her little nudges here and there towards it. But she's also kind of shy. I'm sure it will happen if you two spend more time together," Val replied.

"This is weird," he said.

"Why?" Lara asked, grinning.

"It's just kind of weird that you're trying to hook me up with another woman," he said, looking at Evie, "and it's weird that you're trying to hook me up with your best friend. I mean, not *bad*. Just weird. But I get it, it makes sense. I know you want me to be happy, Evie, and having sex with Lori would certainly make me happy, and you want Lori to be happy, Val, and you know I'm a safe bet for that."

"Honestly, yeah. It's hard to find a guy who's a safe bet. Not just to show you a good time but to not try to force you to do something you don't want to do. I can break guys in half if I want to, but Lori can't. And I'd rescue her in a heartbeat and rip some shithead's fucking head off if I had to for her, but I can't always be there. But based on everything I've seen, you're clearly a safe bet. You wouldn't fucking *survive* trying to abuse most of the women I've seen you hook up with."

"Yeah, that's true," he replied. "Ellie would rip my throat out, Lara would break my neck..."

"Cait would straight-up murder you," Evie said.

David laughed. "Yeah. But I'd never do anything like that anyway." He frowned as he considered what lay ahead of them. "Lara, you said this place was in stalker territory. I know we've reduced their numbers, but...how bad do you think it could get?"

She sighed. "Fuck, I really don't know. Given the shit we faced during that initial campaign against them, well, you know how bad it could get. I mean, based on what I saw, there were dozens of stalkers hanging around back then. There could be hundreds, or none. That's why I had us load up on guns, ammo, and explosives."

"Yeah," he murmured. He'd come equipped with a pistol on each hip, his assault rifle slung over his shoulder, and a double-barrel sawn-off shotgun in a holster on his back. Cait had gotten him into the habit of wearing one every now and then just like her. He'd gotten pretty good with his quick-draw, though she could still easily outdraw him. His pockets were heavy with magazines and a single grenade. They didn't have a lot of them, given how hard they were to come by nowadays. The others were similarly decked out.

"We'll be ready," Val said. "I've handled shitloads of stalkers before. I mean it's always a gamble, but I think you're all pretty good. I mean, you'd have to be to still be alive this long. I've seen some of you fight now, too."

They fell silent as they hit the mountain and began swinging around it, following a rough trail between its base and the edge of the woods. David couldn't help but wonder if they might run into Lima Company, as this was fairly close to their territory. He'd meant what he said earlier to Val, that he didn't think they would seriously do anything against them, but...he couldn't shake this sense of unease he got whenever he thought about them.

He wondered how Catalina was doing. He hoped that she was okay.

The group moved across the landscape, scanning the trees around them and the mountain above them. David had been admittedly reluctant to stick near the mountain path, as although it was the quickest route there according to Lara, it also meant that they were open to attack from above. Hunters hung out near the mountain.

Or at least he'd been assaulted by some while here earlier. But the skies were clear for now, and besides a few zombies lurking among the trees several dozen meters away, there didn't seem to be anything stalking them in the forest.

They managed to hold onto their luck for another thirty minutes.

And then the problems began.

As they came around the mountain and plunged into a large forest that contained the abandoned logging mill, David began to pick up the subtle and creepy hints that they were being hunted. By stalkers.

He caught flashes of movement around them, heard the occasional sound as the incessant chirping and buzzing of insects fell away around them. Soon, they were moving more slowly through the woods, following a rough animal trail southeast, caught in a bubble of silence that was broken only by the occasional movements of the undead around them.

"We've got company," Val muttered.

"Yeah, this is definitely stalker territory," Lara replied unhappily.

"There's a clearing up ahead," David said. "I say we get to it, wait for them to come to us. Lara, how far are we?" he asked.

"Maybe ten minutes," she replied.

He grunted. That could be a very long ten minutes, and that was just getting there. They hurried up and hustled through the trees to the clearing. As they approached it, the activity around them increased. Based on what he'd learned over the past year, David thought that maybe there were a few dozen out there at least, possibly more.

They made it to the clearing and established a defensive perimeter, waiting.

They didn't have to wait for long.

Three stalkers appeared in his field of vision and he could just barely make out more on the edges of his perception. They raced forward, reaching with clawed hands, sharp tooth-stuffed mouths open and eager for fresh meat to feast upon. Val and Lara both called out 'Contact!' at almost the same time and then

David was firing. A burst of bullets from his assault rifle cut through the air and ripped into the lead stalker.

It punched ugly holes into the thing's neck and face, shredding it and spraying the trees and other stalkers around it with gore. They ran faster, shrieking wildly, a shriek that was picked up and echoed by the others around them. They were surrounded. David released another two bursts of gunfire, the gun rattling in his hand, but even as they were cut down, more were already appearing.

David kept calm, forcing himself to stay focused on taking them out and putting them down as quickly as he could manage. He shifted aim and fired once more, then repeated the action, and again until the gun ran dry. He'd downed nine of the fuckers but still more were coming. With quick, precise motions he reloaded, took aim, and kept firing.

The others fired their own weapons around him, and stalkers shrieked in every direction in rage and pain as they were put down like the monsters they were. Gunshots and wild screams echoed across the forest as the firefight continued. David blew the head off one with a well-placed spray of lead, shot out the chest of another, and then he was out again and reloading once more. The seconds slammed by as he emptied his assault rifle a third time. Blood flew on the gun smoke-stricken air as the corpses stacked up.

He was halfway through his fourth magazine when the last stalker he could see fell and no more appeared. For a few seconds, all he could hear was heavy breathing and reloading. A few more shots rang out over the next minute or so as a few stragglers arrived or survivors made themselves known, and then they were finished.

"I. Fucking. Hate. Those things," Evie growled.

"They are quite awful," Akila agreed.

David glanced at their nymph friend. He had to imagine that she hated them the most out of all of them, as she had the most reason to. Although he had no particularly powerful distaste for the zombies that were his own kind rendered undead, (if anything he preferred them as they were the least lethal of all the variants), he knew that her entire clan had been brutally murdered by or converted into stalkers. They had ripped her life to bloody shreds, and quickly, too.

"Let's get a move on," Val said.

They picked it back up, hurrying out of the clearing and setting a fast pace through the woods. More stalkers began to appear as they drew closer and closer to the logging camp, and they were each put down with a quick headshot snapped off every time one appeared. David became convinced pretty quickly that they were simply heading deeper into what was heavy stalker territory, and it filled him with dread.

The last time they'd seen *this* many stalkers around…

He derailed that train of thought, preferring to focus on the moment. Finally, after just about ten minutes, they came through a treeline into the edge of a large clearing. And there it was: the logging mill. It was surrounded by a chainlink fence rusted through in several places, collapsed in several others.

He saw a handful of structures within. He stared at the buildings, expecting to see at least a few stalkers lurking, maybe crawling up the sides or across the roofs, but he didn't see anything. Immediately, he became suspicious.

"Now what?" Akila murmured.

"We go in, nice and easy," Val replied.

They set off, keeping their place slow but steady, constantly searching for more hostiles. A pair of buildings, what looked like a trailer to their left and a bunkhouse to the right, was the first on the list. There were another two trailers in a row with the first, a pair of sheds beyond the bunkhouse, and a larger building dead ahead, on the other side of the camp.

"Akila with me, we'll search the trailers," Val murmured. "David, you, Evie, and Lara check the bunkhouse and the sheds. Grab what you can. We'll meet near the middle of camp and then take on that last building. Sound good?"

"Sounds good," David replied, and the others murmured agreements.

They split up. David led Evie and Lara slowly across the overgrown ground. It was obvious that a lot of stalkers had come and gone, and sometime recently, their strangely shaped feet printed obviously into the mud from the recent rains.

There was something horribly, disturbingly familiar about this whole scenario, but he prayed that it wasn't what he thought it was. With great caution, he approached the bunkhouse and opened up the door. He expected the worst as he peered in, assault rifle at ready, but nothing dangerous greeted him.

Shafts of sunlight slanted in through the broken ceiling, dust motes dancing among them. They illuminated a room of old beds, mostly just skeletal metal frames, some still sporting mold-covered mattresses. Dirt and trash covered the floor and the wood he could see was warped heavily by no doubt years of rain and snow getting in.

"Will you watch the door?" he asked, looking at Evie. She nodded. He and Lara headed into the derelict structure.

They moved slowly among the ruins, checking beneath and around the furniture, though there wasn't a whole lot to see. David poked his head into one of the few doors at the back of the building, finding an old shower area half-covered in plant life that had gotten in and proliferated. He listened for signs of life as he hunted through the area, but all he could hear were the sounds of Lara investigating nearby and nothing else.

In his mind's eye, he could envision dozens of stalkers creeping steadily forward from the woods around them, surrounding them in perfect silence as they prepared to launch an all-out assault.

He shook off the dark thoughts and quickly finished up his search. As he suspected, there was nothing worthwhile in the bunkhouse. Decades of wanderers and prospectors had picked the place clean, and he hoped that this wasn't entirely the case, but knew it was always a possibility. They stepped back outside with Evie.

"Anything?" she asked.

"Nothing," David replied.

They pressed on. David led them to the nearby pair of sheds, tossing an uneasy glance out to the forest beyond the fence and the clearing surrounding the encampment. He glanced over as he saw Val and Akila moving onto their own second structure.

Val held up something, a tool, and gave a thumbs up. Well, that was good at least. They'd found *something*. The ominous silence and foreboding tension persisted as they reached the first shack. They split up, Lara taking one, David taking another, while Evie stood guard again.

He stepped inside, checking out any hiding

places a stalker or anything else could theoretically be concealed away in. The place was vacant of undead, but he liked his chances for finding one of the tools he was looking for.

He spent the next ten minutes intensely focused as he hunted through the handful of crates that were scattered through the dirty interior of the shed, keeping an ear open for any trouble as he worked. In the end, he managed to track down just one of the tools they were looking for, in this case an axe. It was in somewhat shitty condition, but Jennifer knew how to fix up tools, so he slipped it carefully into his pack.

He stepped outside, finding Lara already out and standing guard with Evie. Val and Akila emerged at roughly the same time and they all walked forward to meet in the center of the camp. Still nothing moved around them.

"How are we doing?" David asked.

Everyone reported in on what they had found. Altogether, they'd found four of the six tools that Jennifer had demonstrated for them, and ideally they should be finding duplicates of some of the tools as well.

"Looks like we've got to search the big building," David said glumly, staring at it. Although he knew in his heart that they'd have to anyway.

"Let's do it, nice and easy," Val replied.

The group set off across the open space in the center of the camp. David readjusted his grip on his rifle again and rolled his shoulders, trying to relieve the tension that was building in him. The structure ahead of him was somehow even more ominous than the water filtration plant had been. He wasn't sure he'd have been able to go in if he had been alone. As it was, even with the women around him, he still had to make himself approach the front doors. They remained silent as the group came to stand before them.

Evie and Val went to pull open the large doors, while Akila covered their back and Lara and David took up aim at the doors, in case anything nasty was waiting beyond them. The two women pulled them open, and the hinges creaked with a horrendous loudness in the still air. They all winced, expecting an explosion of activity to burst into existence, but yet still the ominous tension persisted, unbroken.

A large, open room, broken in half by a huge piece of machinery, awaited them. There was nothing immediately threatening that David could see, though he didn't relax as they secured the doors in place. Slowly, he and Lara moved inside, each covering half the huge room. Immediately, an awful scent hit him, a terribly familiar one.

"David..." Lara murmured.

"I smell it," he replied, already hunting for the source.

Lara found it first. She said his name again, and the fear in her voice immediately made him turn towards her. There, off in the far corner, he saw it.

"Holy shit, what is *that?*" Val muttered as she and Evie came in behind them.

"It's a stalker nest," Lara replied. "Jesus fucking...I had hoped to never see one of those goddamned things again."

David found himself nodding silently as he stared at it. He didn't want to believe this was what they were walking into, but here it was.

"Why aren't they attacking us if we're this close to their nest?" Val asked softly.

"I don't know," Lara replied just as quietly. "It

was wildly inconsistent when we were bombing them before. Sometimes they'd attack before, sometimes they'd attack while we were laying the explosives to take them out, sometimes they didn't attack until after we blew the charges. And we never figured out what determined that."

"What should we do?" Evie asked uncertainly.

"I thought this might happen," Lara said. "So I brought some explosives with me. Whatever we do, we *have* to destroy this place."

"Agreed," David said. He sighed, considering it. Looking around, he spied a platform midway down the huge piece of machinery that divided the large room in half. "Val, climb up there on that platform and keep an eye on everything. Everyone else, stay on this side of the building and hunt around as fast as you can for tools. If we can make it, I want to finish the search, then we'll plant the bombs and get the fuck out of here. If we get attacked partway through, we'll all focus on protecting Lara while she sets the bombs, *then* get the fuck out of here. Good?"

They all responded positively. Val headed over to the platform and clambered up onto it. Once she swept the area and gave them the 'all clear' signal, they got to work. The group moved to the right side of the building, opposite where the nest was, and quickly began their search. The next several minutes passed with an almost unbearable tension as they hastily hunted through a pair of small storerooms, a break area, and what might once have been a repair area. They tried to find a balance between being quiet and being fast.

Luck, it seemed, was with them. For now at least. They managed to track down the rest of the tools they needed, a few duplicates that would make the process of producing lumber go faster, and even some other intact tools and spare parts that might be useful in other applications. After securing everything, they returned to the main area.

"Anything?" David asked.

"If there'd been anything, you definitely would've heard about it," Val replied. "Are we good? We gonna blow this place to hell?"

"Yes," Lara replied. "Stay there and keep watch. Everyone else, with me. Be prepared to run like hell back the way we came when I give the signal."

"Got it," Val said.

They moved slowly along the machinery in a group, more tense than ever as they approached the nest. It was just as hideous and terrifying as David remembered them all being: an ugly collection of rotting vegetative matter and, in some places, what he thought were corpses. Or parts of corpses, human and animal mixed in. He shuddered. What a fucking awful thing to have to be near. As they got close enough to it, Lara shrugged out of her pack, carefully crouched down as she swung it in front of her, then opened it up and began pulling out the explosives she'd brought. It was probably close to the last of what they had left.

David got into position as Lara set to work. He knelt and aimed his rifle back down the way they had come, between the wall that held the entrance and the machinery in the center of the building. Evie and Akila positioned themselves closer to Lara, watching her. He searched for signs of the stalkers, knowing that at any second it could all go to hell and they could come screaming out of every opening in the building.

There were several windows, almost all of them

broken out. For about a minute there was only the sound of Lara working and the others breathing, and his own heart hammering furiously in his chest, his blood pounding in his ears.

He tried to make himself relax, but after everything that had happened during the initial campaign against the stalkers, he knew it could get really, really bad.

"Contact!" Val snapped at the same moment David both heard a sound near the door they'd initially come in through and saw a shadow fall across the floor in front of it. She fired and something issued a shriek that got cut off abruptly.

And then it was like the ripcord of a chainsaw being pulled as utter chaos revved up around them. Stalkers immediately began appearing in the windows all around. He heard a roaring shriek behind him but didn't have time to deal with it as he sighted one of them scrambling in through the nearest window.

They all opened up at the same time, utter chaos being loosed. David sent a spray of bullets towards the creepy undead monster and they ripped into it, knocking it back out the window in a burst of blood and gore.

Almost immediately another one appeared in its place, scrambling to get through the broken window, cutting itself on the glass still left in the frame. He shot it in the head, killing it and causing it to get stuck there. He shot the next one that tried to climb over its corpse and blocked the window as he killed the third creature.

More were coming in through the other windows. Val was cutting them down as fast as they were coming through the open doors, and behind him Evie and Akila were murdering even more of them.

David emptied his first magazine and hastily reloaded. They were getting through the windows faster than he could kill them, dropping down onto the floor, where he shifted his aim as he finished reloading. He moved fast, letting his reflexes do their job. Readjusting his aim, he popped two shots into the face of another stalker coming at him and then shifted the muzzle to the right, releasing a quick, controlled burst and nearly decapitating another stalker as it landed and straightened up. He repeated this action again and again, squeezing the trigger and aiming with a smooth precision. The second magazine bought him eleven kills.

"How long?!" he snapped.

"Almost done!" Lara replied immediately, raising her voice to be heard over the chatter of the quartet of weapons and the shrieking of the dozens of stalkers.

More were appearing all the time. He wondered how they were going to get out of here. Well, that was a problem for a moment or two from now. David kept firing and rattled through another two magazines mowing down as many of the monstrous things as he could, desperate to keep them back from himself and those around him.

"Done!" Lara snapped.

By the time she'd said that, an idea had come to him. "Get back behind the machinery in the middle of the room! I'm throwing a grenade at the door!" he shouted.

He finished off the current magazine and then pulled out the single grenade. He waited two seconds, then pulled the pin and tossed it as the others got behind cover. He imagined that if the grenade was going to potentially set off the explosives, Lara would have warned him, but she remained silent, so he threw it and then rushed to join the others. David just managed to get behind cover and start reloading before the grenade blew.

"Go!" he screamed, his ears ringing from the explosion.

Whipping back around, he got a look at the way ahead. A dozen and a half stalkers lay in bits and pieces, scattered across the floor. The front entrance had been blown out, parts of the wall missing, a few bits on fire. Good, the whole building could burn for all he cared. Well, in about a minute it *would* burn, burn and explode into a million pieces. He sprinted over the corpses as the others came after him. They burst back out into the sunlight and prepared to make the run across the camp, back towards the mountain.

But what he saw made him hesitate.

There were dozens of stalkers out there, and they were all recovering from the explosion, either from damage it had done them or shock it had delivered to them.

"We gotta punch a hole through them," Val growled as she stepped up next to him.

"Yep." David raised his rifle and opened fire. The others joined him, standing in a rough line and hosing the enemy down with five different blasts of bullets. He pulled the trigger until there was nothing left in the gun and quickly reloaded. As he did, he heard a different shrieking roar coming from his left. Snapping his head in that direction, he felt his heart skip a beat as he spied a dark tide of rippers making their way over and through the fencing.

There had to be thirty or forty of them.

"Oh come *on!*" he screamed.

"Go! Go! We need to get the fuck out of here!"

Lara yelled.

They ran down the rough corridor of space they'd opened up for themselves, between where they stood and the entrance they'd initially come in through. Wounded and dazed stalkers beset them on either side, but they were quickly shaking that off. Thankfully, as the rippers surged into the camp, it only confused things even more, because they had to get through the stalkers on that side to get to the survivors in the middle.

And the stalkers weren't having any of it.

Immediately the two undead groups fell on each other, brutally ripping into each other with tooth and claw. Meaning they largely had to deal with only those left on the right. David twisted, aimed, and fired as he kept on running, pegging several stalkers that had regained their feet and were coming after them. He fired controlled bursts as accurately as he could until his gun ran dry and then he was reloading again. The others were doing the same, and they managed to keep the stalkers off of themselves long enough to hit the outer perimeter.

"I'm gonna blow it!" Lara said as they ran towards the forest.

"Do it!" David replied.

She had the detonator in her hand.

She hit the trigger.

What felt like a powerful, warm hand suddenly shoved directly into David's back and he was sent stumbling, falling and rolling a few times as a tremendous roar tore through the area and a hot wave of air blasted over them. He felt strong hands on him within seconds and Val and Evie helped him up to his feet.

He saw Akila helping Lara up as well. As they

kept running, flaming debris raining down from the sky, he glanced back over his shoulder. There were still a few lingering figures among the flames, but they didn't seem in any condition to follow.

David turned back and kept running into the forest, eventually slowing to a brisk walk.

All in all, a successful operation.

CHAPTER ELEVEN

"Oh yes, this is *exactly* what I was looking for," Jennifer murmured as she inspected the tools they'd laid out for her on a table set up in the shadow of the building she was currently working out of, a small shed in the backyard of one of the houses at the new settlement.

David felt relieved as she said that. It would be a real pain to think they'd gone through all that for nothing. Well, not for *nothing*. Even if it was a bust otherwise, they had still managed to wipe out a stalker nest and kill dozens upon dozens of stalkers *and* rippers.

That was always a positive.

"Good," Val said. "How long before you think we'll be able to chop down some trees. Because I was thinking it would be nice to augment our fence with a wooden one, or at least be able to build a few watchtowers."

"I still need to get the water running, but after that, I should be able to clean up these tools for use within a day or two. After that, I'll need to train people on them."

"How do you know this stuff?" Lara asked.

"I worked at a logging site a few years back. One that was still running. The guy in charge was old, probably seventy, and his dad had run such a site and been teaching him all about it, so he knew his shit. People still needed wood for building after the end of the world. I was a fairly quick study so I worked the machines and repaired them in exchange for a place to live for a little while. It's not like we'll have a full production site, obviously, but these tools will help. I think we could have a watchtower or two up within a week or so. A good, sturdy one, better even than the one we built back at Haven."

"Good to hear," David said. He yawned and then popped his back, relieving some tension. "Goddamn, I need a nap."

"You'll want to get a full night's sleep for tomorrow. Ellie took a walk up to Haven while you were gone to check in and grab some supplies I needed from my place, and they told her the farmers had been by. Your truck is ready to go," Jennifer said.

"Well all right, I guess we'll head out first thing in the morning," Lara said.

"What will you do?" he asked to Val.

"Head home for the night, check in with Lori," Val said.

"She's at Haven," Jennifer said, looking up from her tools. "She stopped by here maybe two hours ago. Came with a small group of people who had gone back to get some supplies of their own from the hunting lodge. She said she wanted to see the progress, and after I gave her a tour, she decided to pay Haven a visit, said she'd wait for you there."

"All right, then," Val said. "I'm ready if you are."

"We'll be back tomorrow night, ideally with a shitload of construction material," David said. He gave Jennifer a hug and a kiss. "You're doing a really good job here," he murmured as he held her. "I wanted to tell you that. And how much I appreciate it."

"I...thank you," she replied, caught off guard. She laughed softly. "I'm just glad to be a part of something like this."

"I'm glad you're a part of it, too."

They kissed again, and then he tracked down Ellie and Ashley. They were in one of the cabins and had just finished having sex, it seemed. He gave each of them a hug and a kiss as well and updated them on the situation.

"You want me to come tomorrow?" Ellie asked.

"Yeah, I would like that," he replied. "Going to need our best shooters for this one, I think."

"Expecting trouble?" Ashley asked.

"No more than usual, but...well, you know how bad 'usual' can get."

She sighed unhappily. "That's fair. I guess I can go another day without you now that I've had you. Just...come back in one piece."

"I fully intend to," Ellie replied. "I'll be at Haven in the morning."

"See you then."

He headed back out to join the others and they began heading back to Haven.

...

They returned home to find April, Cait, and Lori in the process of preparing dinner. The group came inside and joined them, helping make a big meal of vegetables, potatoes, venison and rabbit. As they did, David heard Lori gasp and he turned around to see her staring down in the corner. He followed her gaze.

"There's...a mouse in here," she said quietly.

"That's Frostbite," David replied. He tore off a little piece of venison they'd finished cooking and had set to cool on the counter and slowly approached. "He's our pet."

"You have a pet mouse," she murmured.

"Yeah. He's been with us since winter."

"He's fucking adorable," Cait said.

"How do you feel about mice?" David asked as he stopped a few feet away and crouched down.

"Fine, he just...startled me. I didn't expect to see a mouse today. I guess I've come across enough of them." She laughed. "He is pretty cute."

Frostbite scurried over to David's hand and crawled into it, grabbing up the venison and beginning to chew on it.

He squeaked, and Lori laughed again.

"You want to pet him?" he asked, running his fingertip gently over the mouse's head, between its ears.

"Uh...yes," she replied.

"Approach slowly and crouch down," he said.

She made her way gradually over as Frostbite ate the meat. When she reached them, Frostbite looked up alertly.

"It's okay," David murmured, running his finger down the mouse's back, along its soft, bright white fur. "Don't worry, it's fine."

Frostbite seemed to agree with this assessment and simply sat there in his palm. Slowly, Lori crouched and extended her hand. She put a finger out and ran it across the top of Frostbite's head, then down his back. She repeated this several times. The mouse squeaked softly and relaxed further in David's hand.

"This is wonderful," she whispered. "He's so cute. And soft. So he's really your pet?"

"Our self-sufficient pet," David replied. "He lives in the walls but I've seen him outside sometimes, scampering around. We feed him every now and then when he comes out and asks, but sometimes whole days go by without an appearance, so he knows how to take care of himself. He's more like a tenant than a pet, I guess."

"How's he pay rent?" Val asked, watching from across the room.

"He makes appearances and is adorable for us," Cait replied.

"I guess that's fair rent. Does he get into the food?"

"No. We keep it locked up pretty securely, but I've never found him somewhere he isn't supposed to be," Evie replied.

"Good tenant," Val murmured.

After another moment, he'd apparently decided he'd had enough, issued another squeak, and then hopped off David's hand and scurried back to a hole in the baseboard. Lori laughed softly, watching him go. David glanced over at her. He hadn't really been this close to her before. Her bright blonde hair was pulled into a ponytail, and she was sporting a healthy tan. Up close, he could see a scar on her face, two actually.

One on her chin, another by her temple, partially hidden by her hair. He could see a few signs of aging, some wrinkles gathering gently at the corners of her eyes, and a weariness there. Though when she turned her soft brown eyes towards his, sensing his gaze, something passed between them, almost like a spark.

She blushed suddenly and cleared her throat, standing up.

"Dinner smells good," she said, rejoining the others.

David stood and glanced at Val, who was just smirking at him. He thought of something to say, then thought better of it and went back to helping finish up dinner. Once it was ready, they served it up and all gathered around the table. He ended up having to eat most of his dinner with just one hand because at one point near the beginning Cait simply held onto his hand and wouldn't let go. Not that he particularly wanted her to.

"I honestly am having a difficult time believing what I've seen so far," Lori said as they dug into their meals. "I mean, I got the impression that you all were competent, but that you've managed to do as much as you have in the time frame that you have is just...it's very impressive."

"To be fair, we have a strong support base, a healthy stockpile of supplies, and practice with this kind of thing," Cait said. "And we've been lucky so far. Luck determines a lot. That's something I've had to learn the hard way."

"Yeah," Lori murmured. "That's true. I honestly just hope that our luck holds out. This all feels like...it's what we've been waiting for."

"I hope it is," David said. "You've all been through so much."

"Yep," Val agreed. She had managed to convince Evie to give her a bottle of wine and let her have half of it, though he imagined Val was going to try, and maybe succeed, to get the whole bottle, given the rate she was going through it.

As they kept eating, he noticed that Lori kept looking at him, those soft brown eyes turning his way repeatedly. And each time he caught eyes with her, she quickly looked away. From the way Evie, Cait, *and* Val were smirking, he knew that they were all picking up on it. He wondered if he was actually going to hook up with Lori, if she was actually interested. He trusted Val's earlier words, and she seemed like she was into him.

As they chatted on and off over dinner and the food disappeared and the conversation eventually dwindled as the sun left the sky, David decided that maybe this time he should be the one to make the move, instead of having one of his girlfriends, or Lori's friend, jump in for him. Normally he was content to have someone make a move on him, but he would actually like to make the first move every once in a while.

"So, Lori..." he said, and he saw Val's eyes widen and she actually leaned forward a little bit. He had to hold back a laugh. She was at the very *least* tipsy.

"Yeah?" Lori asked.

"You want to spend the night?"

She licked her lips, glancing briefly at Val, then back at him. "With you?"

"Yes," he confirmed, "with me."

She looked again at Val. "I would, uh, I'd like that," she said. She paused, looking around at the others. "You mean sex, right?"

Val laughed loudly. "Oh come on, obviously!"

"Yes," David said, understanding how she felt, "I do mean sex. Here, tonight, you and I."

"I want that," she replied. She looked around again. "Given that you're all smiling, um...we're all good with this?"

"Yes," Evie said.

"Mmm-hmm," Cait murmured, smiling, and April nodded, as did Akila and Lara.

"Anyone else who should be, uh, informed? I saw you getting handsy and kissy with Ellie earlier," she murmured.

"Ellie's fine with this," David said.

"Okay, good, because I don't want a woman like

that coming after me in a jealous rage. She looks like she could take my head off," Lori muttered.

"She could," Cait said.

"She could try," Val murmured.

"I would *hate* to see any of you fight," David said. "I mean, for obvious reasons, but also because it would certainly be brutal. Although I *am* kinda curious who would win in combat."

"I would," Akila said.

"Against who?" Evie asked.

"All of you."

Val sat up straighter and fixed her with an intense gaze. "Oh yeah?"

"Yes. Based on my observations of you all, I have superior reflexes, and a tremendous amount of pure survival experience. One-on-one, I'm convinced I could take you all. Not that I would *want* to by any means."

"Maybe you and I should go one-on-one tonight in your bedroom," Val said, still staring at her with an excited interest.

"I accept your challenge," Akila replied immediately.

"They *are* talking about sex, right?" April asked uncertainly.

"I'm not sure *they* know," David replied.

"Come on, let's go," Val said. She stood up and tossed a glance to Lori. "Enjoy yourself, he's a *great* fuck."

"So you *did* fuck him!" she said. "You said–"

"I didn't say one way or the other. Whatever you chose to believe is your business," Val replied as she began following Akila out of the room.

"Don't break anything! And don't be too loud!" Cait called.

Neither woman responded as they left the room.

"Is there, uh, anything else we need to discuss?" Lori asked in the ensuing silence.

"I don't think so," David said, looking around.

"Can we watch?" Cait asked eagerly.

"Oh. Um..." Lori hesitated.

"It's okay if the answer is no," Cait said.

"It's not that I don't like being watched. Well, by people I like. And I do like you all. It's just...I really want the very first time to be, um, intimate. And alone."

"That's fine," Cait replied.

"I don't mind if you watch a second time, and honestly..." she bit her lower lip, "I was hoping to see you and David in action. Watching extremely close couples having sex has always been a huge turn-on for me, *especially* if someone is pregnant."

"Sure!" Cait replied.

"She looks *amazing* naked."

"And better getting rammed by David," Evie murmured.

"She *does* look good taking his dick," April agreed with a small smile.

"You all do," David replied, making the others laugh.

"Of course you'd think that," Lara said.

"Well then, I'd *really* like to get to the sex," he said, standing up and walking over to Lori. He offered her his hand. "Shall we?"

"Yes," she said with a small smile, "we shall."

She took his hand, got up, and let him lead her upstairs. A wonderful chill of excitement shivered through him as they walked up the stairs and into the bedroom. He was going to make love with Lori. She was very beautiful, but more than that she was clearly a strong, competent woman, though had a curiously shy and somewhat anxious exterior. He could see, in a way, why Val provided such a good foil to her, being hard when it was required.

"Wow, that is a very big bed," Lori murmured as they came in and he closed the door behind them.

"Yep. Evie and I custom made it when we first moved into this place. Figured we were going to need a big bed simply because she's seven and a half feet tall. Then Cait ended up joining us every night not long after we realized she was pregnant. And more often than not someone else will find their way into the bed for the night. Usually Lara or Ellie, but sometimes Akila or April or even Jennifer," he said.

"So you *have* been intimate with Jennifer? You've had...sex, with her?"

"Many times," he replied.

"Interesting. Uh, not that I have anything against that, or her, I just...I wasn't sure if wraiths even wanted to have sex anymore. Some of them I've come across, if the topic was broached, said they just didn't care about it anymore."

"I think it depends on the wraith. No two wraiths are exactly alike and it seems like the infection targets random things. Some don't need to breathe, some don't produce heat at *all,* some go deaf, some can still eat, some can't. Some are still horny, some aren't. Jennifer was really horny in the beginning, but after I, uh, satisfied that urge enough, I think she realized she had been trying to sort of 'catch up' on all the sex she hadn't been having, and that she was comfortable with a much lower amount." He walked over to the basin and began stripping. "We can clean up here."

"Oh, right," Lori said, joining him.

She stared at him as he peeled his shirt off and

began undoing his belt.

"Wow," she whispered.

"What?"

"You are in *really* great shape. I mean, most people I come across are in decent shape at least, because this lifestyle demands it, but you are...quite nice to look at."

"Thank you. So are you," he replied as she took her own shirt off.

She laughed as she kept stripping. "I've always known that I was attractive. I tried not to let it go to my head, but it was hard. Guys kept wanting me, offering, asking after me. It was nice...you know, when it wasn't, like, aggressive. More than once I've had to cut someone who didn't know when no meant fucking no. And for a while I thought I was...well, just fantastic. And then I met Val. Personally, I think she's beautiful, in a daunting sort of way, but it's clear that she isn't what you would call traditionally attractive."

She took her bra off after getting her pants, boots, and socks off. Her tits were really nice. Beautiful, firm c-cups with nice dark pink nipples. "Given the fact that you've fucked her, I'm guessing you agree that she's beautiful."

"Oh yeah. She's...something else," he replied.

She laughed. "Yes. She is. But after I met her, and saw how just...effective she was, how self-confident she was, I don't know, it changed my view for some reason. I'm embarrassed to admit it, but it made me reconsider the importance of charisma. I knew I wasn't just attractive, I knew how to convince people to do things. I thought I had a leg up on most everyone else. And I do, in some ways, but so does Val, in completely different ways. She's just *so...*intense! So effective. So powerful. She's like a force of nature. We're all alive because of her."

"I'm sure you had something to do with it," David replied as they finished getting naked.

"Maybe," she murmured, looking down at his cock, which was mostly erect by now. "Don't take this the wrong way, but I thought you were going to have like a monster cock."

He laughed. "Why?"

"Partially because of all the women who willingly and openly lust after you and sleep with you, but mainly because of Evelyn."

"Oh, yeah. I think Ellie said the same thing. Or something like 'so that's the dick that satisfies a goliath, huh?'"

"I mean, again, I think it's fine. It's great, actually."

He laughed. "Great?"

"I mean, I think so. What, should I have said amazing?" she replied, taking her panties off.

He paused, glancing at her vagina. She had a nice little bush of blonde hair. "No," he replied, "and, did you trim?"

She glanced down briefly and laughed. "Is it that obvious?"

"No, I mean...normally the women I know just shave it off. Sometimes they trim."

"I hadn't for months," she replied. "I figured...Val pushed me towards something like this, said you'd probably ask to hook up soon, so if I was gonna be, uh, presentable, I'd better do it sooner instead of later. I'm glad I didn't wait. I didn't quite expect it to be tonight."

"Did I jump the gun?" he asked.

"No, no, it's fine. Honestly, it was a pleasant

surprise."

"I'm glad. As for my dick, I've never been impressed by it, so it surprises me whenever women seem to like it. I mean, looking at it. Well, feeling it, too."

"Honestly, if it was much thicker, we might not have been able to do it."

"Well, glad I'm not too big then," he replied.

They each grabbed some soap and rags and began washing up.

"I have to admit, I was a little afraid I'd come up short myself," she murmured as she washed up.

"How so?" he replied.

"I mean, like I said, I've known I was attractive for most of my life, but...good lord, David. Cait is just...out of this world. She is *so* beautiful, she's fucking drop-dead *gorgeous*. And you're the father of her child, you're in love with her. You must fuck her every day. And she just looks like someone who's *really* good at sex, on top of being phenomenally attractive. And then there's Evie and April, they're both really pretty, and fuck, Ellie, Lara, Akila, you sleep with them all, too, and they're all just amazingly beautiful..."

"Lori," he said, and he stepped up behind her, setting his rag and soap aside and then settling his hands on her hips. He put his lips near her ear. "You're beautiful," he said, and she shivered and exhaled sharply. "I love them all in my own way, and they are all remarkably beautiful, each in their own unique way, and yes, most of us fuck a lot, but don't compare yourself." He slipped his hands up her smooth, wet body, cupping her breasts and gently massaging them, making her gasp. "All that matters right now is you and me. Right now, there's no one else. You don't ever need to compare yourself. I think you're an amazingly sexy woman."

"Oh my," she whispered, shuddering as he ran his fingertips across her nipples. "That's-oh shit!" He slid one hand down, and lower, until his fingertip slipped between the taut lips of her vagina. He found her clit and began to massage it gently. "Ah! Oh wow, David. You are...holy shit, that's...oh wow." She moaned and shuddered in his grasp as he began fingering her and kissing the side of her neck. "Holy shit this is so hot," she whispered. "You are something else. Good lord. I just-ah!-I can't-oh fuck!"

"Shh, Lori," he whispered and began kissing the other side of her neck.

She was reduced to moaning and crying out, letting him hold her up as he continued groping her breast with one hand and pleasuring her with the other. He kissed her neck, the sides and the back, where she seemed particularly sensitive, listening to the sounds of sexual pleasure. It didn't take long for him to make her come.

She let out a strangled cry of bliss and her whole body went rigid, then convulsed a few times as she began to orgasm. He'd gotten a finger up inside of her and he could feel her vaginal muscles clenching, a hot spray of sex juices coming out of her, leaking down her firm thighs and making a mess he'd have to clean up later, not that he cared.

When she was finished, he took his finger from her and just held her, hugging her from the back, listening to her gasp and try to speak.

"That was...intense," she whispered. Gently, she pulled herself from his grasp and then turned around. Looking up at him, she kissed him suddenly, hard on the mouth. They began to make out and he kept groping her, first her breasts again, then down to her ass, cupping it, finding it firm but pleasantly padded, smooth and soft, fitting perfectly into his grasp. She reached between them, her hand finding his rock hard cock, gripping it.

Suddenly she broke from the kiss and dropped to her knees. He watched, breathing heavily now, as she slipped his cock into her mouth and began bobbing her head, slobbering all over it, sucking him off like a skilled prostitute, her lips slipping up and down rapidly as she stared up at him. It was amazingly wonderful to see this woman who, until several minutes ago he had only known dressed up and as a leader, nude and on her knees, putting his dick in her mouth. It was amazing, having heard the sounds of ecstasy she had uttered as he'd pleasured her.

Something he had suspected when he'd first seen her was confirmed just then: she looked *really* good sucking his dick.

Although, he had to admit, he had yet to encounter a woman who didn't look good sucking his dick.

She sucked him off for about a minute before spitting a gob into her fist and beginning to massage the head with it, making him groan and stagger slightly from the unexpected burst of extra pleasure it gave him.

"Can you fuck me now?" she asked, panting a little.

"Uh, yeah," he replied. "We can move over to the–"

"No," she interrupted him, glancing back over her shoulder at a table next to the washbasin, "here. Right here."

He grinned. "Okay."

She stood up and moved over to the table, then hopped up onto it. As she spread her legs for him, he stepped up to her.

It was at perfect fucking height.

"You've fucked a lot of women on this table, haven't you?" she asked, noting the blanket and pillow that were already on the table for, well, just this occasion.

He laughed as he stepped closer to her. "I mean, not *too* many..."

She gripped his shoulders, staring at him with an intense lust. "Don't fucking lie to me, David. Tell me."

"Eight," he replied.

"Oh wow." She smirked. "You just knew that immediately. Anyone I'm not familiar with?"

"Just one," he replied. "One from the hospital crew."

"You're a very bad boy, you know that?" she murmured as she reached down and gripped his cock. She began to rub it gently against herself.

"Sometimes," he agreed.

"Just one thing," she said, relaxing slightly, looking more annoyed than anything. "Two things, actually. Um, pregnancy..."

"I managed to get my hands on some birth control after I accidentally knocked Cait up. So we're solid there," he replied.

"You're sure?"

"Yes. Trust me. If it didn't work, there would be at least one other noticeably pregnant woman around here," he replied.

"Hmm."

"Second thing?"

"Go slow. It's been a while, and you're...thick."

"I won't hurt you," he replied, and kissed her.

She moaned and kissed him back intensely. David began working his way carefully into her wonderfully slick vagina. She gasped and moaned as he penetrated her, spreading her legs out wide and then gently resting her heels on his lower back while also gripping his shoulders. She looked down between them.

"Holy shit I forgot how hot it can be to watch a dick go inside me," she whispered.

"It's pretty great putting it in you," he murmured, looking down with her, watching himself disappear slowly into her, pushing gently deeper, pulling out, fucking her at that depth for a bit, then carefully working his way in.

"You're-ah!-you're good at this," she whispered. "Nice and smooth...oh wow. I really have forgotten what sex is like."

"It's really good," he replied, already losing himself in her. He looked up. "Before I get too lost in you: do I have to pull out or can I let off inside you?"

"You can go inside me, I don't mind," she said.

"Oh fuck, good."

He kissed her and pushed himself the rest of the way into her. She moaned into the kiss and then cried out as he really started fucking her. And then he *was* lost inside of her, lost inside that perfect, hot, tight wetness, that pocket of divine bliss. He lost himself in the simple, primal joy and satisfaction of fucking an attractive woman, of exploring her wonderful body for the first time. David found himself staring into her eyes, feeling an intense spark of lust and connection between them, and then she kissed him once more.

He slipped his tongue into her mouth and she

moaned, twisting and twining their tongues together, running her hands over his body. He returned the favor, groping her wonderful breasts, then sliding his hands down to her great hips.

Lori was in wonderful shape.

After a bit, she released him, with her hands and lips at least, and laid back on the table. She secured her hold with her legs on him a bit more tightly as he began driving into her roughly. "Oh *fuck!*" she cried, then placed her hand over her mouth. "God, you're making me loud! There are so many people around..."

"I guess you'll just have to be quiet," he replied, watching her wonderful tits bounce in sync with his thrusting. He reached down and laid a hand against her lower belly, settling his thumb over her clit. Her eyes went wide.

"No, I can't–" she began, then cried out as he began to rub her clit while pounding her deep and hard. "Please! I can't help it!" she groaned, trembling.

"I could help," David replied.

"How...?" she moaned, panting.

"You into being restrained at all?" he asked.

The way her eyes flashed told him all he needed to know. "Kinda," she admitted.

He smiled, then clapped his other hand over her mouth. "Shut up," he replied. "Shut your mouth, Lori."

Then he started fucking and fingering her harder.

She bucked hard against the table and let out a shriek against his hand. She kept yelling as he continued pleasuring her.

"Shut your fucking mouth, Lori," he growled at her and she let out a deep, muffled moan.

Within seconds she was coming again.

David groaned in response, experiencing that

wonderful feeling of tight, hot, wet vaginal muscles growing hotter and wetter as they fluttered and clenched and spasmed around his rigid dick, bathing him in pure pleasure.

He started coming before too long. Both of them moaned and writhed and twisted in absolute bliss as they orgasmed together. He shot his load into her, draining his cock into her fantastically tight pussy, pumping her full of his seed in hard contractions.

Each time his cock jerked inside of her, spurting a fresh blast of his seed out, a pulse of hot pink ecstasy exploded inside of him, growing in power each time until finally he was just dry-kicking and there was nothing left to give. He continued rubbing her clit until she had finished coming, then he pulled his hands away from her and settled them on the table to either side of her head.

Panting, he stared down at her. She looked more beautiful than ever, her blonde hair a wild mess, her face flushed, eyes wide, breasts swaying rapidly as she panted, gasping for breath. After a moment, she said, "That's the best sex I've had in fucking ages."

"I'm glad," he replied, then he leaned down and kissed her on the mouth. "You deserve it, Lori. You've worked so hard and been through so much."

"God, I can *really* see why so many women jump on your dick every night," she murmured, reaching up and hugging him to her, kissing him several times. "Fuck, I'm jealous."

"Well, if you're going to be living around me, there's nothing saying this can't be semi-regular," he replied.

"That is *exactly* what I need in my life. Some guy I'm really attracted to who's good at sex and I can just fuck every now and then and he won't try to tie me down."

"That's me," David said, straightening up. He stretched and yawned, popping his shoulders and then his neck, then he pulled out of her.

She laid her hand over her vagina. "Will you get me a rag? It feels like you came *so* much."

"Yeah," he replied, wetting a rag and then passing it to her. "I do that, apparently. If you'd like, I can get Cait."

"Yes, although...could we cuddle for a bit?"

"Of course," he replied.

Once she'd cleaned herself up, he called down to Cait that he was about ready, and then they laid down together on the bed. He laid on his back and she laid half on him, her slowly cooling body feeling wonderful against him. Cait, Evie, April, and Lara all appeared not much later.

"You used the table didn't you?" Cait asked, grinning.

"Yeah," Lori murmured sleepily.

"Is it okay if we're all in here?" Evie asked.

"Yeah, I don't mind. How could you tell? About the table?"

"Heard it banging against the wall," Lara said. "David's fucked all of us on that table when we just can't stand waiting and need it *right* away." She glanced at Evie. "Well, just about all of us," she amended.

Evie laughed. "Yeah, my huge ass would break that thing."

Cait began stripping. "Ready for a great show?" she asked.

"Hell yes," Lori replied.

...

"Now *that* is a truck," Val said, grinning as they approached the vehicle.

After preparing for the day the following morning and gathering up his companions, David had led them out of Haven and towards the farm. Once they got there, the farmers had taken him to where they had brought the truck: next to the river.

"We figured you'd appreciate it if we got the annoying 'get it out of the farmland' part of it out of the way," one of the men guiding him said.

"Definitely appreciated," David replied, looking the vehicle over. It was of a pretty good size, a flatbed covered in a chipped, pale yellow paint job. It looked like it could haul a pretty appreciable amount of supplies. Which was good, considering at least some of them were going to have to ride in the back.

"Who knows how to drive?" he asked, suddenly realizing he hadn't thought of that.

"I can," Val replied.

"Okay, you drive." He looked around at the others. He'd brought Ellie, Akila, Lara, Jennifer, and Lori, of course, had opted to come along as well. He'd brought Jennifer in case they ran into anything technical or mechanical while investigating the site.

"Who sits up front?" he asked, considering it.

"How about you and Lori? I wanna talk with you two," Val replied.

He glanced at the others, who all seemed open to sitting in the back. "All right."

"Don't worry, it's not like I can really haul ass in this thing. Everyone just get situated and hold on, and you'll be fine," Val said as she headed up towards the cabin.

He glanced at Lori, who shrugged. She'd been

quiet ever since they'd had sex a second time this morning, but it didn't seem like an unhappy quietness. More like a...satisfied one. A serene silence. She took his hand and led him to the cabin.

Everyone got into the truck. Val took a moment to pop the hood and check it over. Apparently satisfied, she slammed it shut and then walked around and looked in the back. Seemingly satisfied a second time, she climbed in front, behind the wheel.

They thanked the farmers and then she began driving, keeping a slow pace down the river. They would head that way until they reached the intersection by the lake, not far from the fishing village, then turn right and head off in that direction. According to the map they were following, that road *should* take them to where they wanted to go, eventually.

"We should be good on gas," Val said. "There's two extra tanks back there and they gave us a full tank."

"That's good," Lori murmured. A few seconds of silence passed. "What'd you wanna talk about?"

"I was just curious how last night went. You were loud."

"*You* were loud," Lori replied.

They'd all heard her and Akila last night. More than once.

Val just smirked. "Yeah but that's no surprise." Her expression sobered suddenly and she glanced at Lori from behind a pair of sunglasses she'd donned. "I just...want to know that you had a good time. You've put up with so much over the past few months. Shit, over the past few years. Running away from disaster sucked by running the town wasn't always a walk in the park either. You've sacrificed so much for us."

"So have you," Lori murmured. Val just shrugged. Lori took David's hand again and laced their fingers together. "I had a fantastic time. David was both a gentleman and...a not-so-gentle man," she said, smiling and blushing.

"Oh yeah? I always thought you liked it rough," Val said, her smirk returning.

Lori sighed. "You have no subtlety."

"Why does that keep surprising you?"

"I don't know." She squeezed David's hand gently. "Rest assured, it was the best sex I'd had in, God, years. But more than that, I felt respected. Listened to. Appreciated. I felt...beautiful. I felt sexy. I felt—" she hesitated.

"What?" Val asked.

She glanced at David. "I don't want to make you uncomfortable."

"I don't think you will," he replied.

"Fine. I felt loved."

"Good," Val said. "You deserve it."

"I-I'm not saying that I'm in love with you or that I think you're in love with me," Lori murmured, looking at him.

"It's okay," he said, laying his hand over the back of hers. "I understand. I...I'm still figuring out what that word means, too. I love several women in my life, in different ways. I think it's fair to say that, last night, there was love of some sort. Don't worry, you aren't stepping on anyone's toes," he explained.

She looked relieved. "I'm glad." She sighed. "I've loved the people under my leadership I suppose in the way a compassionate leader can love their people. But the only person I've loved beyond that for a long time..." She glanced at Val.

"I love you too, Lori," Val said easily.

She smiled. "You're my best friend. Ever."

"Same."

David glanced at them, thinking about what Val had said earlier, about wanting to hook up with Lori. Maybe he should try to make that happen.

"So...now that we've gotten to know each other better, uh...threesome?" he asked.

Lori looked at him in surprise. "What, the three of us?" she asked.

"I mean...yeah."

"I'm down," Val said.

Lori blinked again and twisted her head to stare at the larger woman. "*Really?*"

"Yeah, why does that surprise you?"

"I just-I...never...I didn't think you thought of me like that," she stuttered.

"If the answer's no, that's fine. We can keep fucking him separately," Val said.

"It's not no, it's just..." she blinked a few times. "I haven't done much with other women," she said finally. "I...like women. I..." she blushed fiercely, "I fooled around with Xenia once."

"Oh really? I thought so," Val said, grinning.

"Yeah, it was...we were tipsy and stressed and she offered and I just...wanted to try it." She looked at Val again. "You never offered."

"I didn't want to make you uncomfortable. Normally I can tell about people, but I couldn't tell about you."

"Tell what?"

"If you'd be okay with it. I didn't want to fuck up the friendship."

"Well, I...appreciate that." She laughed softly. "This is a surprising turn. Um. Okay. Sex...with the two of you. I...need more time."

"Take all the time you need," Val replied. "If the answer's no, that's fine. We can drop it."

"I'm sorry if I made you uncomfortable," David said, "I just thought...you two seem like you'd be good together, you know?"

"I'll just have to think about it," Lori replied.

"Okay."

He'd taken a gamble, he knew, but she didn't seem angry or upset, just surprised. Kind of pleasantly so. Well, he imagined it would be nice to learn that your best friend, who you've been attracted to for some long length of time, is actually okay with having sex with you. Or he hoped that's how it was going.

He felt confident Lori was sexually attracted to Val, and obviously Val was to Lori.

They fell into silence, with Lori leaning her head against his shoulder and letting him loop an arm around her, holding her against himself, as they drove on.

CHAPTER TWELVE

David had spent most of his life walking.

Or running.

Sometimes there was a lot of running involved. But he had spent at least some of the time in vehicles. By the time he climbed into the truck and was driven across the countryside beneath the rising sun, it had probably been three or four years since he'd done so. It took some getting used to. It was kind of scary, once Val picked up speed.

Although she didn't go over twenty miles an hour most of the time, given the shit state of the road and the fact that they had people in the back, it was still so much different than walking. But eventually he got used to it and watched the miles roll past.

They drove down a road that was dirt for a while, then became gravel, and eventually gave way to cracked pavement. Val navigated them with a smooth confidence, driving them around obstacles and past a number of derelict structures.

Eventually, the pavement gave way to gravel again, and after nearly two hours on the road, they saw the structure that the map indicated. It was a large, half-completed building that sat at the edge of a gravel parking lot, joined only by a handful of rusting vehicles and a trio of trailers in a line.

"So that's it, huh?" Val murmured as she pulled up in the parking lot.

"Looks like it," David replied. "Let's get this show on the road."

"Yep," Val said, killing the engine and hopping out.

They all dismounted and took a moment to

stretch. David took the opportunity to check the area out, trying to anticipate any problems. There weren't obvious signs that there were any threats in the area, human, inhuman, or undead, but that wasn't always a certainty. The way to the right let onto a rolling field that eventually led to a lake.

It was big, open, and obvious, and he doubted any threats would be coming from that direction. Or at least threats that still had brains for tactics. To the left and ahead, however, the trees grew right up to the property, so that was pretty easy for cover for anyone or anything that might want to attack.

"Lara, Ellie, check out the trailers and see what you can find. And maybe keep an eye on the truck. Everyone else, with me," David said.

They all nodded and set to it. He led Val, Lori, Akila, and Jennifer to the main structure. It was a curious thing, a three-story building that was half-finished, the back of it, the way facing them, completely open to the elements. Judging by the piles and piles of bricks and other material, he imagined that it hadn't been that way initially and that weather and time had brought the back wall down.

It was strange being able to see into the structure like that. The third story looked like it hadn't gotten much work on it done, but what he saw on the ground floor seemed promising. Lots of crates, lots of tables, stuff under faded blue tarps.

They moved through the open-faced back and set to work, first checking out the area for anything that might be lurking. They moved through a large room that was probably intended to be the entrance lobby for whatever the building was going to become when it was finished, they moved into a short corridor that ended in some stairs, leading up and away to the left and right, and checked out a pair of doors occupying the corridor.

One led to a room that was completely empty, the other led to a room stuffed with more supplies, though it was obvious that someone had gotten into it at some point, and that this place might once have served as someone's temporary home. After they cleared it out, they regrouped in the corridor.

"Akila and I will check out the next two stories. Why don't you all see what you can find in these crates," he said.

"So you *do* take charge," Val murmured with a small smirk.

"Yeah?"

"I was wondering if you were gonna."

"Get to work," he replied.

She laughed. "Don't push it."

"Yes ma'am."

While Val, Lori, and Jennifer began opening crates to see what kind of supplies they'd found, he and Akila headed upstairs.

"You are a strange man," Akila said as they searched through what there was to search of the second floor. It had partially collapsed, and judging from what he saw above them, almost all of the third floor had collapsed.

"What? Why?" David replied, surprised. Akila was generally a silent woman. If they were working together, sometimes they could go whole jobs without sharing a word. He'd been a little put off by it at first, but he'd eventually learned that she just didn't say much sometimes. And he'd become convinced that she liked him well enough by this point.

"In my experience, those who lead often do so for their own sake. They claim to care about others, and perhaps that is true in the beginning, but...many of them lie. People want power for the sake of power. But I believe you. Not just because of your words, but because of your actions. You have consistently proven that you care about other people. You will suffer for them. And not just those closest to you. I have seen you working in the hot sun, laboring these past several days for people we did not know at all before last week," she explained.

"What do you make of that? I know some people who would say that is a weakness."

"I do not agree with that assessment. I admit, I am more hesitant to help, though less so since having met you and the others at Haven. You have shown me a kindness I did not know outside of my clan. Perhaps even among them, in some ways. A kindness I have never known. I think reasonable measures must be taken, but in general, most people could do with being kinder. I like this about you. It is...a very attractive quality. If it were possible, I might have one day asked you to...be the father of my child," she murmured.

"Oh. Wow."

They had just finished their search of the second story, finding a little more supplies and nothing hiding in the area. He thought they were really alone now, at least in the building. He looked at her as they approached the stairs to the third floor.

"I am sorry if that was inappropriate."

"No, no, not at all," he replied, taking her hand. "Honestly, that means a lot. I would have helped you, if I could. Do you want a child?"

She sighed. "I do not know, to be honest. Now? No. But someday? Perhaps." She smiled. "You are going to be a great father."

"I hope so," he murmured.

They headed upstairs and cleared out the third story. There was nothing up there, and it was a dangerous place to be anyway, the floor having given out in most places.

"We should get back down and help the others," he said as he turned around and began heading back towards the stairs.

But Akila was standing near one of the windows, still as a statue. "David," she said, her voice quiet, flat, full of danger.

He swallowed, immediately feeling a buzz of adrenaline hit him.

She had seen something.

Gingerly, he joined her, keeping his movements slow. Coming to stand by his nymph friend, he looked down and felt his heart freeze in his chest.

He saw a dozen dark shapes in the forest, waiting. They were not undead, he realized. Initially he had mistook them for rippers, but they couldn't be. They were still and silent, and as more appeared, he saw that their movements were too smooth, too intelligent.

"The ones Val spoke of," Akila whispered, drawing the scoped rifle she had taken with her for this trip. "The ones in black leather."

"No, go downstairs," David said, drawing his own rifle. He had kept his loadout from the logging site, and now he was glad. "Warn them and then get outside and around, see if you can get behind them. And, please, be careful."

"I will." She hesitated only for a second, then gave him a quick kiss. "If I don't come back, know that I love you inasmuch as I've loved anyone."

And then she was gone.

He blinked and felt real fear on top of surprise. Akila had never said anything quite like that to him. That she had just done so meant that she was very nervous about their odds. Shit. He carefully got into position.

They hadn't noticed him yet, he didn't think. He made sure his magazines were easily reachable, that his rifle had the safety off, and that he was in a good position. He stood a foot back from the window, as much as he could manage and still look down, just able to see the row of them. God, there were twenty of them now.

Were there more that he couldn't see?

Fuck!

He'd have to move forward if they charged, but for now–

They began moving into the clearing between the building and the forest. Fuck! Fuck! Now or never, David realized.

He opened fire.

The first volley was good and he was glad that the situation appeared so obvious in what it was: they were coming here to murder them. All of them were armed, all of them moved with a lethal intent, all of them wore that ominous black leather armor. As his attack took down two of them, racing for the building, their response was swift and precise.

The ones running began falling back, the ones who had stayed behind at the treeline immediately targeted him and opened up with bursts of automatic fire. David cursed and fell back, barely avoiding getting his head blown off. Goddamn, they were quick, and good.

Almost immediately more gunfire came from below him, cutting down another four of them trying to make it back to the woods. He shifted to the right, where another window was, aimed out of it and fired, hosing the enemy down and trying to confuse or at least frighten them with the bullets. He emptied the magazine and saw that he at least managed to hit a few others, but then another concentrated burst of gunfire reached out for him. As he fell back, groping for another magazine, he felt a round come terrifyingly close to his face.

As he reloaded, he heard more gunfire come from the right side. Ellie and Lara. He shifted over to a window overlooking their position and saw gunfire coming out of the doorway leading into one of the trailers, and a window in the same trailer.

He also saw movement behind the trailer. Heart hammering, David took aim and fired, putting a round through the head of another one of the warriors in dark armor. There were six in total and the others immediately began to respond. He kept firing, knowing he couldn't let them attack Lara and Ellie from the back. Another went down as they began to return fire, and then another, taking a few lethal shots to the neck. Gunfire peppered his position. David cursed, ducked, and came back up, aiming and firing.

They were good, they were really good, but he had been training his fucking ass off and he'd gotten really good at snap aiming and accuracy with this weapon. His scope sighted on one man's sneering face and he squeezed the trigger. The face disappeared in a spray of gore and he flopped back, dead. David yelled as a burning line of pain cut across the top of his left shoulder and he dropped to one knee, ducking down. Grimacing, he glanced at his shoulder. A bullet had winged him. Ignoring the pain as best he could, he shifted towards another window, deeper into the third story. The floor creaked and groaned ominously beneath him.

He popped up and opened fire again. There were just two of them left now. One was aiming at the trailer, the other was aiming at David. All three of them fired at the same time. David's burst connected with the body of the man firing at him, throwing his aim off and knocking him to the ground. Another shot took him in the face. But the last survivor was now emptying his magazine into the trailer where Ellie and Lara were. David grit his teeth, shifted aim, and emptied his own magazine into the fucker.

When he was done, there was nothing left but a badly chewed up body with a heavy spray of blood all around it.

David went to reload, noticing that gunfire was not coming out of the window now, only the door. Goddamnit. He shoved a new magazine in, turned to head back to his original position, then froze as he felt the floor shift beneath him. As he was preparing to make a leap back to safety, the floor gave out completely and a scream was torn from his lips as he fell down to the second story. He landed with a solid and ugly sound as he smacked into the floor. Pain assaulted him as the rifle flew from his hands, his breath driven from his lungs.

He'd landed on his side and one of the pistols had been driven into his hip, digging cruelly into his body. Gasping and moaning weakly, he tried to get back to his feet. Yet still more gunfire raged all around him. Looking around, he tried to find his assault rifle, but he couldn't. Cursing weakly, he pulled one of his pistols out and slowly shifted to the nearest window. He had to keep in this fight. Every bullet counted.

David got to another window, wheezing and wincing, forcing himself to look past the pain that now wracked his body, and grimaced at what he saw. There were now something like twenty corpses spread out along the field and the treeline. His allies were doing good, but there were still more attacking them.

How long could they keep this up? David took the opportunity for this moment of surprise to take aim and fire at two he could see clearly. His first shot was accurate, punching through a woman's forehead and killing her instantly. The man next to her immediately readjusted the submachine gun he was holding and began to fire. David kept firing, two shots punching into the man's chest armor, then another into his neck.

He ducked down and cried out as another shot winged him, ripping skin out of his left bicep. Immediately he could feel hot blood trickling down his arm. Cursing, he blind-fired out of the window while waiting for the pain to subside.

Shifting places as bullets ripped through the area around him, thankfully mostly stopped by the brickwork of the building's exterior, he reloaded. He could hear Val shouting something below. As he finished reloading, he heard running footsteps coming up the stairs not far from him.

Preparing for the worst, he took aim, then relaxed as he saw Jennifer emerge.

Her eyes widened as she saw him and rushed over. "David! You're bleeding!"

"I know," he groaned. "Just grazes. I'll be fine. Where's Akila?"

"She slipped out the back to swing around behind them. Come on, there are more attacking from the left. That's why I'm up here," she said, a grim expression on her face.

He nodded and forced himself to his feet. They shifted through the second story until they came to the empty windows overlooking the left side of the area. A dozen men and women in black armor, some of them human, some of them inhuman, were hurrying across the field. David and Jennifer stepped up to two different windows and opened fire, raining down death from above. Immediately, they began to both return fire and retreat. David ducked, narrowly avoiding get shot yet again, and then kept firing.

Right as he began to run out of ammo, something completely new happened. One of the men he was watching, who had almost made it back to the treeline, suddenly snapped back with a spray of blood and brains escaping his head. A man next to him skidded to a halt, raising his rifle and aiming into the treeline, and immediately met with a similar fate.

Akila.

She must have made it behind them.

With Akila's help, hidden somewhere among the trees and foliage, he and Jennifer quickly cleaned up the group that had been trying to attack them from the side. They moved back over to the front and David felt another sick pulse of fear blast through him.

The survivors were rushing the building, and whatever resistance the others below them were offering wasn't enough.

"David! Jennifer! *NEED BACKUP! NOW!*" Val screamed at the top of her lungs.

"Go for the stairs," David said, remembering a hole in the floor he'd seen earlier that might be able to get him into a position to get the jump on them, as he saw a few of them breaking around the sides. She nodded and raced off. Checking his pistol, he ran off deeper into the building. He could hear more gunshots, shouting, running footsteps. Holy fucking shit this was getting out of control. Skidding to a halt, he came to the hole in the floor. It offered a view down into the main room they'd initially come in through.

A shadow fell across the floor where he was looking and he took aim. A second later someone in black leather armor appeared and he fired, capping the fucker in the head and killing them instantly. Almost at the same moment, bullets began punching up through the floor around him as others nearby returned fire. Cursing, he tried backing up while also returning fire, shooting wildly into the floor ahead of the hole.

The floor beneath him groaned and gave way.

Not again! He thought angrily as his stomach dropped out and he crashed to the first floor. He kept firing as he fell, aiming as well as he could amidst the chaos. He heard someone shout as one of his bullets connected and then he slammed into the floor yet again. Gasping, he blinked rapidly in the dust that swirled around him.

There, two figures ahead of him. He aimed and fired.

The pistol clicked empty.

Without even thinking about it, he dropped the gun and quick-drew his sawn-off. Aiming right as one of the figures stepped closer and prepared to end his life, he squeezed the trigger. The shotgun was like a cannon going off, his arm jolting painfully as the shell exploded out of the muzzle and blew the head clean off the hostile. Again, without thinking about it, he reflexively snapped the gun to the left and repeated the action.

The second attacker fell, equally headless, a tremendous spray of blood splattering across the ceiling overhead.

David dropped the shotgun as more figures appeared, coming in the same way they had initially come in through the missing back wall. He drew his second pistol and opened fire, still laying on his back, fighting viciously to keep his cool and his concentration as yet still more pain battered his body relentlessly. He began squeezing the trigger, missing as often as connecting, and put down three of the four that had come inside.

He began reaching for a magazine to reload as the fourth drew a bead on him and knew he didn't have time to reload.

He thought of Cait. And Evie. And April.

The man's head snapped back right as his finger tightened on the trigger, his right eye turning into a bloody explosion.

"David!" Lori yelled.

"I'm fine!" he growled as he took the time granted to him to reload. "Help the others!"

"Are you sure?" Lori replied somewhere behind him.

"Yes! Go! I've got the back!"

She didn't respond. He listened for retreating footfalls, hoping she had fallen back to help Jennifer and Val, but he couldn't hear much with all the gunfire he'd endured recently. His pistol reloaded, he snatched up his shotgun, cracked it open, and shoved two more shells into it. Waiting for more assholes to show up, he slowly worked his way backwards, trying to get to the safety of the hallway if at all possible.

No one else showed up.

As he moved back, the gunfire slowly died off.

Almost a minute later, as he made it to the hallway and waited, watching the rear, he sensed as much as heard heavy footfalls coming up behind him.

"David," Val said. "Are you okay?"

"Fine," he managed. "The others?"

"Lori and Jennifer are okay," Val replied. "I took a shot in the arm but it went through. I'll be fine. I don't know about the others. It looks like that's the last of them, but we need to be sure." She came to stand beside him.

He nodded and thrust a hand up. "Help me up."

She grabbed him with her good arm and pulled him up. He cried out but grit his teeth and staggered to his feet. "I need to check on Ellie and Lara. Akila's out there, probably making sure none of the stragglers get away."

"Good, I'll go help her. We can't let them report our location." She paused. "Lori! Jennifer!" she snapped. The two women appeared in the hallway.

"Yeah?" Lori asked, trembling, clearly shaken, but still in control of herself.

"Start loading up everything you can in the truck, as fast as you can. David, help them after you check on the others. And keep a sharp fucking eye out. We need to get the hell out of here as quickly as we can," she said.

"On it," Jennifer replied. She patted Lori gently on the shoulder. "Come on."

David and Val left the building, taking a moment to check the rear parking lot and making sure nothing was lurking about. He didn't see any dark shapes. Val set off to the left of the building, where the strike force had attempted to get inside before getting caught in the crossfire, and he left her to it.

Somewhere, a gunshot rang out. Akila, hopefully. David raced off towards the trailers. The gunfire had been coming out of the middle one.

"Friendly, coming up!" he called as he jogged over.

No response. Fuck. He headed up the few stairs and in through the front door, taking in the interior of the building with his gaze, and yet again he felt cold, awful fear snap into him as he saw Lara on the floor and Ellie crouched over her.

"What happened?" he asked, hurrying over.

Ellie was tending to a wound in her right thigh. "She got shot," she replied curtly.

"I'm okay," Lara replied tightly. "Fuck, David, you got shot, too."

Ellie glanced briefly at him, then went back to work.

"Just a few grazes," he replied.

"Are the others okay? Please fucking tell me they're okay," Lara groaned.

"They're all fine. Lori and Jennifer didn't sustain any damage. They're loading up right now. Val got shot, but she's still going." He paused. "I guess I don't know Akila's condition. She ran out into the woods to flank them." He paused again as another gunshot went off. "I think that's her. She's picking off stragglers."

"Good," Ellie grunted. She yanked on something and Lara screamed. "Sorry."

"Fine," Lara gasped. Ellie stood suddenly. "Do what you need to do, I've stabilized her. I'm going after Akila and Val to help make sure the fuckers can't report back our position." Before either of them could say anything, Ellie had already raced out of the trailer, hefting her pistol.

David crouched by Lara. She was sweating and pale, she looked awful and there was a lot of blood. "I'm sorry," he whispered. "I saw them attacking from the back and I tried to kill them before they could shoot the place up. But...I didn't manage it."

"It's fine," Lara replied. She pointed at her backpack. "There's local anesthetics in my medical pack. Find them. It'll help with the pain."

He nodded and hurried over. Digging through her pack, he pulled the kit out, cracked it open, and began sorting through it. A moment later he had what she wanted. He moved over to her leg and injected her carefully a few times around the wound.

Before long, she let out a sigh of relief.

"It went through, thank God," she whispered. "Hate having to dig around in there."

"I'm sorry," David replied.

She grabbed his hand. "David, look at me. I'll be fine, okay? You did excellent, I'm sure. I've been shot before, okay? You've seen the scars. I'll be fine. Just...help me up, back to the truck. I can't carry shit, but I can stand guard. But first patch yourself up."

He hesitated, then nodded. "Okay."

David took the minimum amount of time required to quickly clean and tend to his wounds. Once they were sealed up, he finished prepping for the move.

He was still shaking from fear and anger, but mostly adrenaline, as he packed her backpack up once more, then helped her up. Carrying the backpack in one hand while using his other to support her, he helped Lara limp out of the trailer. They passed Jennifer on the way over to the truck. She stopped, having just dropped something off, and gasped.

"Oh, Lara," she whispered.

"I'll be fine, keep working," Lara replied.

"I...okay," she said, nodding and hurrying off.

"You help them. I'll watch the truck," Lara said.

"Okay."

David helped her into the back, got her situated, made sure she had ammo for her weapon, and then hurried off.

They were right, they needed to get the fuck out of here.

...

Half an hour was all they dared spend at the construction site.

David, Jennifer, and Lori hastily grabbed as much construction material as they could, going for what they thought they needed the most, and also wouldn't be able to find easily elsewhere or make for themselves. Lara guarded the truck. Of the three who had gone out to hunt down the survivors, Val returned first.

Grimacing, she was carrying an armful of rifles. She reported that Ellie and Akila were still out hunting, and she was going to gather as much in the way of guns and ammo as she could from the dead bastards.

After another fifteen minutes, Ellie and Akila came back. Silently, they helped gather the weapons and then, once they'd stripped what they could from the dead bodies, they helped load the construction supplies. Once they had gotten as much as they were going to, they refilled the truck's tank with gasoline and prepared to leave.

"We found a survivor," Ellie said as they gathered for the last time around the truck.

"What'd they say?" David asked, intrigued despite everything that had happened.

"Not much. He was dying. They call themselves the Marauders. He said they're going to find us, and they're going to kill or capture everyone, and there's nothing we can do about it. We might as well give up and make it easier. Because there's a lot more of them," Ellie said.

"We shot him after that," Akila said flatly.

"Did any of them make it away?" Val asked.

They both looked uncomfortable. "We can't know for sure," Akila replied. "I don't think so, but this is a wide, open space and there were a lot of them."

"Great," Lara muttered.

"Well, we had to travel a ways to get here," David said. "Hopefully they won't be able to track us. But...either way, we need to get home."

"I *would* like that," Val replied.

They got into the truck. Val, David, and Lori got into the cabin again, this time Lori taking on the role of driver.

David couldn't help but feel a sense of foreboding as they began driving back home.

EPILOGUE

A week passed.

Though he didn't feel comfortable doing it, David spent the first two days after getting back simply recovering. Mostly in bed with Cait. She would hardly let him leave their bedroom, let alone the main office. His reports came to him from Evie and April, everyone else was too busy. Ellie, Akila, Jennifer, and Ashley were spending almost all their time at the new settlement.

Besides immediately putting the new construction material to work after offloading most of it and then driving the truck and a small portion of the material back to the farmers, they were on high alert. None of them saw any reason not to take the Marauder threat seriously.

According to what he'd heard, they'd warned the hospital crew, the farmers, and the fishing village. They had even sent a runner, (two, actually, for safety), to Lima Company to let them know, although all they'd really said was, 'thanks for the warning', and that had been it. David supposed he should just be happy it wasn't a negative response.

On the third morning, April had reluctantly let him go after tending to his wounds again and he promised that he wouldn't work too hard. On the one hand, he wasn't looking forward to getting back to work. His muscles were still sore, and his body just generally ached from all the abuse it had suffered at the construction site.

On the other hand, he was feeling way too guilty for just laying around while everyone else was working their ass off. Although he felt really bad for

Lara, because he knew it had to be even harder for her.

April wouldn't let her leave Haven at all and Lara was very reluctantly mainly just staying in her room. It hadn't been too difficult at first, given the amount of pain she was in, but that had slowly ebbed away as the days wore on. David visited her often, and usually found Cait or Evie or April keeping her company.

He could tell it was really wearing on her, not being out there. But the good news was that they were getting work done. A lot of it. They put the construction materials to use, as well as the logging tools they'd salvaged from that site, and the more of the area they secured, the more people they were able to bring in to help do more work.

By the time a week had passed, David was feeling better, and they had finally managed to move everyone in Lori's and Val's group from the hunting grounds to the new settlement. They had managed to get a fence up around the rearmost two clusters of buildings and the mansion tucked away on its own private property, where Lori, Val, and some people from Haven, who had yet to be determined, would run the settlement from.

As night fell at the end of that week, a lot of people gathered in the mansion to have a celebration. A huge meal was cooked up, some alcohol was broken out, and everyone spent hours celebrating their hard work as the sun began to go down.

David had been reluctant to agree to Cait coming down from Haven, but she'd been insistent and she had made a good point: she wasn't *that* fragile or incapable of defending herself. After getting Ellie to agree to provide a bit of a guard for her with him, he'd agreed and they'd gone down to the new settlement. Honestly, he felt bad. He didn't want it to seem like he was trying to keep her cooped up in Haven, he just...worried about her. So very much.

It would be so easy for just *one* undead to kill her *and* their child...

But he wasn't thinking of that tonight. The only ones not present from his main group at the mansion were April, Jennifer, and Lara, who were all back at Haven, managing things there. There was a lot to do. They were going to have to decide who would move to this new settlement to help run it, how they were going to divide up responsibilities, what was left on the list of things to do to get the place up to snuff, and a lot more.

But that also could wait.

David had been talking with damn near everyone all night, tired but happy, his wounds finally not aching for once.

By the time the night was beginning to die down, the people preparing to head off to bed for the night, he found himself sitting on a couch not far from the front door with Cait.

"You did incredible work," she murmured as she shifted more comfortably against him.

"I tried," he replied. "It was really hard."

"I know. You've done so much. I'm so proud of you." She gripped his hand and looked over at him. "I want you to know that: I'm proud of you. I knew you were a good man when I asked you to be with me, but...I guess I didn't realize just *how* good of a man you were. You're the most inspiring person I've ever met."

"Really?" he asked, vaguely uncomfortable.

"Yes."

"I...am honestly not sure how to react," he admitted after a few seconds.

"It's okay. I know how you feel. I–"

She froze as someone shouted something outside, one of the gate guards. David's heart skipped a beat as fear flooded his system.

Now what?

"Stay here," he said, standing up and pulling his pistol from its holster. He heard someone arguing outside and headed for the open front door. Before he could get there, a familiar voice shouted out for him.

"David! Lara! They're coming!"

Catalina?

He hurried outside, gun drawn, tasting fear.

He began to call out, to try and figure out what the hell was going on.

That was when something smashed against the side of his head and everything went dark.

ABOUT ME

I am Misty Vixen (not my real name obviously), and I imagine that if you're reading this, you want to know a bit more about me.

In the beginning (late 2014), I was an erotica author. I wrote about sex, specifically about human men banging hot inhuman women. Monster girls, alien ladies, paranormal babes. It was a lot of fun, but as the years went on, I realized that I was actually striving to be a harem author. This didn't truly occur to me until late 2019-early 2020. Once the realization fully hit, I began doing research on what it meant to be a harem author. I'm kind of a slow learner, so it's taken me a bit to figure it all out.

That being said, I'm now a harem author!

Just about everything I write nowadays is harem fiction: one man in loving, romantic, highly sexual relationships with several women.

I'd say beyond writing harems, I tend to have themes that I always explore in my fiction, and they encompass things like trust, communication, respect, honesty, dealing with emotional problems in a mature way…basically I like writing about functional and healthy relationships. Not every relationship is perfect, but I don't really do drama unless the story actually calls for it. In total honesty, I hate drama. I hate people lying to each other and I hate needless rom-com bullshit plots that could have been solved by two characters have a goddamned two minute conversation.

Check out my website
www.mistyvixen.com

Here, you can find some free fiction, a monthly newsletter, alternate versions of my cover art where the ladies are naked, and more!

Check out my twitter
www.twitter.com/Misty_Vixen

I update fairly regularly and I respond to pretty much everyone, so feel free to say something!

Finally, if you want to talk to me directly, you can send me an e-mail at my address:
mistyvixen@outlook.com

Thank you for reading my work! I hope you enjoyed reading it as much as I enjoyed writing it!

-Misty

MISTY VIXEN

HAVEN 7. Copyright © by Misty Vixen.
Paperback Edition. All rights reserved.

This book is a work of fiction. Names, characters,
places, and incidents are either products of the
author's imagination or used fictitiously. Any
resemblance to actual events, locales, or persons,
living or dead, is entire coincidental. All rights
reserved. No part of this publication can be
reproduced or transmitted in any form or by any
means electronic or mechanical, without permission
in writing from the author or publisher.

Made in the USA
Monee, IL
12 January 2024

51672109R00139